(Mis)Reading Different Cultures

(Mis)Reading Different Cultures

Interpreting International Children's Literature from Asia

Edited by
Yukari Takimoto Amos and
Daniel Miles Amos

ROWMAN & LITTLEFIELD
Lanham • Boulder • New York • London

Published by Rowman & Littlefield
An imprint of The Rowman & Littlefield Publishing Group, Inc.
4501 Forbes Boulevard, Suite 200, Lanham, Maryland 20706
www.rowman.com

Unit A, Whitacre Mews, 26-34 Stannary Street, London SE11 4AB

Copyright © 2018 by Yukari Takimoto Amos and Daniel Miles Amos

All rights reserved. No part of this book may be reproduced in any form or by any electronic or mechanical means, including information storage and retrieval systems, without written permission from the publisher, except by a reviewer who may quote passages in a review.

British Library Cataloguing in Publication Information Available

Library of Congress Cataloging-in-Publication Data Is Available

ISBN 978-1-4758-3689-9 (cloth)
ISBN 978-1-4758-3691-2 (electronic)

∞™ The paper used in this publication meets the minimum requirements of American National Standard for Information Sciences—Permanence of Paper for Printed Library Materials, ANSI/NISO Z39.48-1992.

Printed in the United States of America

To our daughter, Himiko (卑弥呼).

Contents

Foreword: The Danger of Cultural Decontextualization in Studying
Diversity through Literature   ix
Geneva Gay, University of Washington, Seattle

Preface   xiii
Yukari Takimoto Amos

Acknowledgments   xvii

Introduction   1
Daniel Miles Amos

PART I: ISSUES AND CONCERNS   5

1. Preparing Our Students for the "Right" Future: Using Children's Literature to Promote Cultural Understanding   7
   Kathy Brashears

2. Authenticity: In the Eye of the Beholder?   23
   Sharryn Larsen Walker

3. Cultural Differences, Interpretations, and Power   35
   Yukari Takimoto Amos

PART II: (MIS)INTERPRETATIONS   47

4. The Cultural Battle between East and West: Chinese *Mulan* Meets Disney's *Mulan*   49
   Annie Yen Ning Yang

5 Remembering the Dark Past: Stories of the Korean War and
   Korean Immigration in American Children's Literature   63
   Chong Eun Ahn

6 Reading with Cultural Empathy: Why Is It Difficult?   77
   Yukari Takimoto Amos

7 Reading Analytically and Feeling Connected: When Indonesian
   Preservice Teachers Read Foreign Stories from China, Iraq,
   and the United States   95
   Tati Lathipatud Durriyah

About the Editors   113

About the Contributors   115

Foreword

The Danger of Cultural Decontextualization in Studying Diversity through Literature

Geneva Gay, University of Washington, Seattle

Many researchers and scholars in different cultural, political, and geographic contexts applaud the power and potential of literature in teaching and learning about diverse ethnic, racial, social, and cultural groups. The argument goes that a people's literature written by and about themselves is second only to direct experience for acquiring authentic knowledge about places and peoples different from our own.

However, this potential can be easily unrealized if or when the contexts out of which literature emerges are ignored, distorted, or unknown. Therefore, using international literature in teaching and learning about ethnic, racial, cultural, and national diversity has much potentiality, but it can also be problematic. This apparent contradiction is explained cogently and from many different cultural and national perspectives by the authors in this volume.

The challenges are not necessarily inherent to the literature itself. As the authors in this book demonstrate, when understood contextually many examples of high-quality children's fiction and folklore from different countries are readily available. Problems begin to occur in the processes of translation or transference from one national and cultural context to another, and when those making the transferences do not preserve the cultural nuances.

Some troubling questions are: Is it always possible to maintain authenticity in cultural crossovers or conversions? What knowledge and skills do translators need to ensure the preservation of cultural authenticity? Is linguistic competency sufficient? If all cultural elements and nuances are not translatable from one context to another, then what?

While it may be true that there are some common themes in literature that transcend national and cultural boundaries, the settings or "spaces" that surround the telling of these stories, and how they are told, are "location specific." These "locations" are much more complex and embedded than merely geographic, temporal, and linguistic; they are culturally nuanced. In other words, virtually all writing (and most certainly the literary genres) is cultural text. The topic and content do not have to be culturally specific to quality as such. The fact that authors are cultural beings and are always *present* in their work, even without deliberate intentionality, makes for writing cultural texts. But because the books that are the targets of analysis in this volume are cast in different nationally based cultural experiences, orientations, values, and perspectives make them even more so.

Given the cultural foundations of the children's literatures profiled by the contributing authors to this volume, even apparently straightforward, literal, linguistic cross-cultural and cross-national translations are problematic. Some words and phrases are not one-to-one conversions from one language to another. In these situations, translators are then called upon to be interpreters and converters, which may shift the nuances of the story and characters and thereby distort their original accuracy and authenticity. Furthermore, authors write for given audiences, both real and imagined.

While translations of literature may not deliberately intend to do harm to the original versions, authors and translators probably want to make their projects reader friendly to marketed audiences, who, invariably, are "culturally located." They may try to make the original works culturally consumable for different settings and audiences, and in doing so they distort the original texts through cultural decontextualization. Even what appears to be a minor structural modification in texts can create major cultural distortions. A case in point is moving from oral to written speech *in the same language.* There are some nuances of vocal communication that simply do not convert well to written communication, and vice versa. Occurrences of mismatches among different languages are even more prominent, and especially so when language translators operate in the absence of adequate cultural knowledge and sensitivity.

These types of cultural incompatibilities as applicable to children's literature are well documented by the authors of the chapters in this book. Their analyses are compelling and persuasive because similar findings are revealed in analyses of translation errors and distortions from a variety of national perspectives, including Indian, Japanese, Chinese, Filipino, Indonesian, Korean, and Thai.

Another important message can be extracted from these chapters. That is, the potentials and problems of translated international children's literature are indicative of broader issues of cultural knowledge, cultural collisions, cultural exchange, cultural sustaining, and cultural appropriation. All of these are serious challenges and opportunities for teaching children knowledge and skills to embrace their own cultural heritages, and to live in harmony and respectfully with cultural others. None of these goals can be ethically and effectively accomplished by decontextualizing various behavioral manifestations, one of which are the stories people write and tell about who they are, how they came to be, and what is of importance to them.

These needs have always been important, but they are becoming even more so as the world becomes smaller and more easily accessible, and the world's population becomes more mobile for multiple reasons and in multiple directions. This means that diverse peoples and their ways of being (cultures, if you will!) are in closer and deeper contact with each other. This plurality offers many enriching and sometimes troubling possibilities. Educators, authors, translators, and interpreters may hasten to try to manage this complexity by reducing it to assumed common denominators and lift humans out of their various contexts. They may try to do so by focusing on claims of human commonality and by creating scripts that symbolize or exemplify this similarity.

This may be another underlying reason why children's literature change meaning when translated from its original language and form into English versions. These culturally decontextualized, translated texts could also be considered as early forms of cultural and intellectual imperialism, inequality, and injustice, especially when they are unidirectional—that is, children's literature translated from other languages and countries into English, but US English language literature rarely being translated into other languages.

These impositions and ways of dealing with international children's literature are certainly at odds with the field of diversity education in its various forms. And it contradicts the human condition—in fact, humans are inherently complex, diverse, and cultural. So, is it not a mystery as to why their creations are likewise complex, diverse, and cultural. They reproduce themselves!

Educators and other professionals could be much more effective and accomplish much more progress in the overall quality of human relationships, interactions, community, and harmony if their service programs and practices routinely reflected and promoted the complex and diverse products humans create without the need to make some better than or mirror reflections of others. Rather, they are different but complementary. Why couldn't these be juxtaposed to each other instead of compared, translated, and appropriated? Why must US authors and filmmakers co-opt and distort *Mulan* by translating their version of it into English? There are women warriors over time who could be studied in conjunction with the story of *Mulan* in appropriate cultural context, such as Trieu Thi Trinh (225–248 CE), who led Vietnamese armies against Chinese occupiers (Nguyen, 2002); or Tomoe Gozen, known for her bravery and strength when fighting alongside male samurai in the Genpei War (1180–1185) (Turnbull, 1987); or Lozen, prophet of the Chihenne Chiricahua Apache, who fought alongside her brother Victorio, a prominent chief, and after he was killed, beside Geronimo when he broke out of the San Carlos reservation in 1885 (Ball, 2015).

Hence, why shouldn't children's literature (or any other cultural artifacts for that matter) from Indonesia, or Japan, or Thailand, or Vietnam, or China, or the Philippines, or the United States, or . . . coexist, be copresented, and costudied in their respective authentic forms and voices? Such a "community of authentic cultural voices" seems a fitting foundation for genuine and egalitarian global citizenship!

REFERENCES

Ball, E. (2015). *In the days of Victorio: Recollections of a Warm Springs Apache.* Tucson: University of Arizona Press.
Nguyen, K. C. (2002). *Vietnam: A long history.* Hanoi, Vietnam: The Gioi Publishers.
Turnbull, S. (1987). *Battles of Samurai.* London: Arms and Armour Press.

Preface

Yukari Takimoto Amos

On one sunny afternoon, Mami, an international student from Japan in our teacher education program at my university, rushed to my office. As soon as she saw me sitting at my desk, she said while gasping for breath, "*Sensei*, it's awful! Americans don't get it!" When I asked her what her mostly white American classmates did not get, Mami began re-enacting a class scene she had just got out of. Calming herself down, Mami continued:

> We read *Faithful Elephants* in a children's literature class. Americans completely ran down that wonderful story. They said that Japanese were unbelievably cruel because they starved the elephants to death. They even said that children's literature books don't need to talk about death!

Faithful Elephants is a story about elephants that starved to death in a zoo in Tokyo during World War II and is widely read by children in Japan. It reminds readers of the wretchedness of the war and both questions and reflects upon Japan's aggressive involvement in the war that affected not only humans but also animals.

Growing up in Japan, various adults—my parents, my relatives, and the teachers at my kindergarten and my elementary school—all read the story to me. I read it myself not only once but repeatedly. Sometimes I was sad and cried. Sometimes I felt totally numb. Of course, I felt for the elephants that died of hunger. However, I have never felt that the zookeepers were cruel and evil. On the contrary, I always empathized with the zookeepers with regard to the difficult decision they needed to make and the concomitant agony they endured afterward.

Therefore, when Mami told me about her American classmates' negative and even harsh reactions to the story, I was in shock. Both Mami and I kept looking at each other's face with the expression: "Why do they read it that way?" We were both speechless. On that sunny day, I was reminded that the ways in which literature is read in one country or culture is not necessarily the same as it is understood in another country or culture.

CULTURAL DIFFERENCES IN INTERPRETATIONS

Five decades ago the anthropologist Laura Bohannan (1966) wonderfully illustrated this point when she described the difficult time she had in recounting a famous story to elders of the Tiv people in Nigeria. Bohannan narrated Shakespeare's *Hamlet* to Tiv elders, but their interpretations were completely different than hers.

To Bohannan's surprise, the Tiv elders were pleased to hear that Hamlet's mother, Gertrude, married Claudius, Hamlet's uncle, immediately after her husband's death. They could not believe that Hamlet's dead father talked to Hamlet as a ghost because, according to their belief, dead men can neither walk nor talk. They were shocked to know that Hamlet attempted to avenge his father's death by killing Claudius, because to raise his hand against someone who had become his father is a terrible crime. Furthermore, they were reproachful of the way Bohannan described Ophelia's death, because "madness cannot drown people, only witches can make people drown. Water itself can't hurt anything." In the end, *Hamlet* was no longer the same story that Bohannan was trying to tell.

In the United States and the United Kingdom, institutional ethnocentrism about international children's literature exists and is perpetuated by the fact that English is a dominant and privileged language throughout the world. This particular type of literature is rarely translated and published in the United States. The proportion of translations of children's literature out of the total consumed in the United States is only 1 percent, followed by the UK at 3 percent. Finland tops the list with around 80 percent of the children's literature consumed there coming from translations. The Netherlands and Italy both are at around 40 percent, while in Germany around 30 percent of children's literature comes from translations (O'Sullivan, 2004).

Obviously, compared to citizens in other countries, Americans and British are not accustomed to reading children's literature from other countries, even in translation. Ironically, while producing the least percentage of translations, the United States and Great Britain provide the world with the most children's literature (O'Sullivan, 2004). In the United States this imbalance between export and import is, according to Stahl (1992), "a form of cultural poverty and testifies to a lack of imagination in an information-rich world" (p. 19).

Because Americans are little exposed to international children's literature when they are young, as adults they may have difficulty in appreciating works that are written from cultural perspectives other than their own.

POWER AND INTERPRETATIONS

Lack of exposure to other cultures was an important reason why Mami's American classmates were unable to appreciate the ways that Japanese understand the *Faithful Elephants* story. They were not accustomed to reading a story from Japan, and thus could not identify themselves with the situations that took place there.

However, my cultural background as a Japanese person made it difficult for me to believe that the lack of exposure alone could produce such harsh reactions to the Japanese story of elephants by Mami's classmates. My own feeling was that the American students' reactions to the story were not only ethnocentric but also tinged with feelings of national and cultural superiority over the Japanese.

Their harsh critique of a story so cherished in Japan evidenced that this was clearly a case of ethnocentrism—the propensity to associate something familiar, in group—with positivity only, and something unfamiliar—out group—with negativity. The Tiv elders were also being ethnocentric when they heard and "corrected" *Hamlet* into their own cultural framework as it was being recounted to them by Laura Bohannan.

However, the American students' ethnocentrism, the extreme negativity they felt toward the story, also possibly originates from the power white Americans feel, in which they posit their ways as normal and valid while viewing Japanese ways and the ways of other foreigners as abnormal, inferior, and even pathological (Taylor, 2006).

Growing up in Japan, I read many stories from other countries in school textbooks and books in translation. However, I don't recall a time when my classmates and I negatively critiqued a story to the degree that Mami's American classmates criticized *Faithful Elephants*. There is a difference in power between Japan and the United States, and it is likely that this power difference affects how Japanese and Americans react to things foreign.

As my coeditor and I discussed this project, we decided that we wanted to explore how international children's literature stories are read in PK–12 classrooms in the United States and are used in teacher education programs in the current era, which emphasizes globalization. International children's literature reflects a country's unique cultural values and practices and is usually not written for people outside the country of origin. Therefore, it is possible that the readers in other countries may misinterpret these stories. Of particular concern is how we read foreign literature within the context of our sometimes unconscious power positionality in the world.

Countries are unequal in the power that they hold. Countries such as the United States dominate others politically, economically, and culturally. Moreover, within countries certain people dominate others because of their race, ethnicity, class, religion, language, gender identity, and other reasons. Focusing on race in the United States, European Americans dominate others. When one group gains social power, it gains the capacity to define sociocultural norms and reality (Taylor, 2006).

In this book we wanted to know how power positionality influences people when they read stories from foreign countries. Ultimately, we wanted to investigate how it might be possible to make Mami's classmates, at the minimum, appreciate the story of *Faithful Elephants*, although they may still not like it.

REFERENCES

Bohannan, L. (1966). "Shakespeare in the bush." Retrieved from http://www.naturalhistorymag.com/picks-from-the-past/12476/shakespeare-in-the-bush.

O'Sullivan, E. (2004). Internationalism, the universal child and the world of children's literature. In P. Hunt (Ed.), *International companion encyclopedia of children's literature* (2nd ed.) (Vol. I) (pp. 13–25). London: Routledge.

Stahl, J. D. (1992). Canon formation: A historical and psychological perspective. In G. E. Sadler (Ed.), *Teaching children's literature: Issues, pedagogy, resources* (pp. 12–21). New York: MLA.

Taylor, J. F. (2006). Ethnocentric monoculturalism. In Y. Jackson (Ed.), *Encyclopedia of multicultural psychology* (pp. 203–4). Thousand Oakes, CA: Sage.

Acknowledgments

This book is about cultural differences in interpretations. In the field of education, cultural differences are frequently discussed in visible forms, such as artifacts, objects, holidays, and customs. However, rarely do we notice differences in the ways we interpret invisible differences. It was Yukari's students from Japan who studied in the university's teacher education program who brought this important issue to her attention. She deeply thanks them for their insights.

Yukari would like to thank Geneva Gay and James A. Banks for introducing her to the topics of multicultural education and culturally responsive teaching when she was a graduate student at the University of Washington. Both scholars treated her, an international student from Japan, just like their other graduate students. She has always appreciated their kindness and encouragement. Despite her busy schedule, Geneva agreed to write a foreword for this volume. She will forever be Yukari's mentor.

Daniel would like to thank the late social anthropologist Barbara E. Ward, his most important mentor during his early days in Hong Kong and mainland China, for her encouragement of his studies and her emotional and intellectual support.

Yukari completed this book while in Hong Kong during her sabbatical, and thanks Central Washington University for granting her the time to concentrate on writing. Daniel gratefully acknowledges the support of the Fulbright Scholar program for granting him funding in Hong Kong during 2017 to 2018 so that he could complete this and other projects.

Shortly before the book project was completed, Yukari and Daniel had the opportunity to present the project to faculty members in the Faculty of Liberal Arts at Thammasat University in Bangkok, Thailand. Thanks are due to Dr. Passapong Sripicharn, associate dean, for arranging an opportunity that provided the occasion to generate useful feedback about the book.

Last but certainly not least, Tom Koerner and Carlie Wall at Rowman & Littlefield deserve great thanks. Their encouragement and expertise in the review and publication of this book was highly professional. In particular, Tom was understanding and patient and provided one extension after another as Yukari and Daniel moved to Hong Kong and took a little longer time to settle in.

Y. T. A.
D. M. A.
Hong Kong

Introduction

Daniel Miles Amos

This book focuses on international children's literature from Asia. After English and Spanish, Asian languages such as Chinese (counting the various Han Chinese languages as one language group), Tagalog, Vietnamese, and Korean are the third, fourth, fifth, and seventh most common languages spoken within homes in the United States. Worldwide, 59.7 percent of the global population lives in Asia (4.5 billion, Worldometers, 2018). Moreover, developing Asian economies have been some of the fastest growing in the world, and by 2014 the purchasing power parity of China had surpassed that of the United States (PwC, 2015).

Despite the prominent role Asian countries have played in the current globalized world, Asian international children's stories have not been widely read and used in US classrooms. This book aims to provide the reader with relevant theoretical frameworks and empirical research findings to address the challenges teachers face when interpreting and teaching international children's literature from Asia. The focus on Asia in this book is ultimately an attempt to make visible the largely invisible nature of power positionality—prevalent in the field of international children's literature in the United States.

The book is divided into two parts. In part I, the book discusses issues and concerns surrounding the use of international children's literature in general. In chapter 1, Kathy Brashears traces the history of the use of international children's literature both in teacher education and PK–12, and she gives the reader an update of the current status. This chapter discusses the scarcity of international children's literature books in the United States, particularly books from Asia, and examines why this is so.

In chapter 2, Sharryn Larsen Walker deals with authenticity issues. First, the chapter explains the differences between international literature, global literature, and multicultural literature. The reader is then introduced to the topic of subjectivity of authors and readers. Walker raises an important question: What does it mean to authentically read a work written by someone whose culture you do not share?

In chapter 3, Yukari Takimoto Amos introduces relevant theoretical concepts and discusses how culture and power influence our interpretations.

In part II, the book explores issues of misinterpretation. In chapter 4, Annie Yen Ning Yang criticizes how Disney distorted the story of *Mulan* in their widely popular movie and analyzes how economically powerful Western societies have used cultural appropriation to transform foreign stories into ones that accord with Western norms.

Chapter 5 looks at children's literature written by Korean American authors. The author, Chong Eun Ahn—a historian—criticizes one-dimensional ways of interpreting the Korean War and its aftermath as depicted by the authors. Ahn cautions the reader to be more attentive to the authors' intent and their interpretations of the historical events, and to read with a greater understanding of historical facts.

Chapters 6 and 7 deal with both conscious and subconscious misinterpretations of Asian children's stories when read by readers who do not share the cultures of the authors.

Chapter 6, written by Yukari Takimoto Amos, presents a research study in which white American teacher candidates interpreted two Japanese children's stories without attempting to reach beyond their own cultural perspectives or positions of power. Y. T. Amos introduces the concept of "cultural empathy" and cautions readers that it can be difficult to surrender your own power to cultural others, even in a sincere effort to read in a culturally authentic manner.

In chapter 7, Tati L. Durriyah takes an interesting turn. Durriyah, an Indonesian Muslim woman professor who teaches in Indonesia, reports her research study in which Indonesian teacher candidates' interpretations of international children's stories from China, Iraq, and the United States were analyzed. Durriyah discusses how our interpretations are intertwined with how our subjectivity is positioned in the world.

All seven chapters are meant for teacher candidates, practicing teachers, teacher educators, school administrators, learning facilitators, and everyone who cares about diversity in general. The book is meant to be useful for those who use international children's literature in the classroom—in particular, literature at PK–16 levels. It is recommended that the accompanying volume titled *Children's Literature from Asia in Today's Classrooms: Toward Culturally Authentic Interpretations* be simultaneously used.

It is our hope that after reading this book the reader will critically analyze their own interpretations when reading literature produced by writers from nations other than their own. When reading stories that originate from countries with different languages, believe in different religions, and hold different values, every reader should ponder where their own interpretations come from.

REFERENCES

PwC. (2015). "The world in 2050: Will the shift in global economic power continue?" Retrieved from https://www.pwc.com/gx/en/issues/the-economy/assets/world-in-2050-february-2015.pdf.

Worldometers. (2018). "World population clock." Retrieved from http://www.worldometers.info/world-population/#region.

Part I

ISSUES AND CONCERNS

Chapter 1

Preparing Our Students for the "Right" Future

Using Children's Literature to Promote Cultural Understanding

Kathy Brashears

Despite what may be a common misconception, the definitions for multicultural literature and international literature are not the same. On one hand, children's multicultural literature addresses books first published in the United States (Tomlinson, 1998) and are about other people and cultures (Iwai, 2013). Tomlinson (1998) demarcates international children's books in the United States as books that are translated and printed in the United States only after they are first published in another country.

Writers of multicultural books write a story about different cultures and groups within the United States, while writers of international books write a story about different cultures and people outside the United States. Goldsmith and Diamant-Cohen (2016), however, assert that when failing to carefully examine books, teachers unwittingly present international children's books as multicultural literature.

Again, although by definition, the terms *multicultural literature* and *international literature* differ, it appears that for some educators the term *multicultural literature* takes on a broader definition, one that encompasses international literature. Whatever our understanding, as teachers, we must be vigilant in recognizing that multicultural children's literature and especially international children's literature are unlike other types of children's books. Specifically, multicultural and international literature offer opportunities for students to consider and understand cultural nuances from perspectives other than their own.

No matter how multicultural children's literature and international children's literature are used or defined, the two types of literature share a common goal—the advancement of cultural awareness in a pluralistic, global society. Such a goal is reflected by Tomlinson's (1998) insight that teachers can foster appreciation for their own culture and that of others by sharing international children's literature with their students.

Although Levin (2007) explains that multicultural literature allows for the use of ethical respect as a multifaceted lens for examining cultural diversity, this comparison is applicable to international children's literature as well. Ethical respect, according to Levin (2017), is just that—respect for others in all aspects of their lives and culture.

Undoubtedly, this type of respect is more easily cultivated in classrooms where students have opportunities to connect with people with whom they may perceive as different from themselves. Such opportunities can be provided through the purposeful use of multicultural and international literature (Iwai, 2013; Levin, 2007; Tomlinson, 1998).

With all this in mind, this chapter will include the history of multicultural and international children's literature in the United States. Also, this chapter will be comprised of a discussion on the identification of international children's literature and the barriers to its publication. Particularly, the need for the inclusion of multicultural and international books within classrooms will be addressed.

In addition, the lack of and need for cultural awareness among preservice teachers will be discussed. Specifically, reasons will be identified that may cause them to avoid or hesitate sharing multicultural and international literature with their students. Finally, the need for educators to develop a plan to use multicultural and international children's books in their classrooms will be considered.

AVAILABILITY OF INTERNATIONAL CHILDREN'S LITERATURE

Unlike in past decades, in the mid-1940s, particularly after the end of World War II, book publishers translated and released a greater number of international children's books than ever before (Lynch-Brown & Tomlinson, 1998). The catalyst for this sudden occurrence may have been the war itself: It brought a clash of cultures to the forefront and, perhaps, made the need to foster appreciation for other cultures more apparent (Lynch-Brown & Tomlinson, 1998).

Undoubtedly, in the 1960s Larrick (1965) initiated another spark of interest in the dissemination of books by publishing companies. Citing evidence from a review of five thousand children's books, Larrick (1965) berated publishing companies, proclaiming that "integration may be the law of the land, but most of the books children see are all white" (p. 63). While forcibly speaking out against the lack of minority representation and primarily focusing on the absence of African Americans in children's books, the premise of her argument may still be relevant today.

Evidence indicates that publishing companies remain reluctant to publish children's literature that features people groups or cultures outside the dominant culture. Case in point, based on a report by the CCBC (Cooperative Children's Book Center), the American Library Association (ALA) (2014) reported that in 2013 only about 5 percent of children's books feature people of color.

While publishing companies lag in representing the large number of different people groups and the shifting demographics in the United States, via technology the world has become smaller (Leland, Lewison, & Harste, 2012). As a result of new technologies, teachers can now readily tap into databases of multicultural and international books and explore customs and cultures across the globe (Leland, Lewison, & Harste, 2012; Yokota, 2009). Undoubtedly, such provisions can provide students with greater opportunities to consider others and develop global consciousness (Yokota, 2009).

Unfortunately, despite the availability or the ease of access to international children's books, studies indicate a limited number of these types of children's books in US classrooms (Leland et al., 2012; O'Sullivan, 2004). In fact, O'Sullivan (2004) points out that US publishers seldom publish books from other countries. This situation creates a need for not only multicultural books but international books as well.

To help guarantee the availability and integrity of international literature, organizations, such as the International Books for Young People (IBBY), were established as early as 1953. Awards are also given to book publishers of this genre, thus promoting the publication of books with potentially controversial, but relevant, societal topics.

While the award may be relatively unknown among teachers (Joels, 1999), the Mildred L. Batchelder Award, established by the ALA, "honors the U.S. publisher of the most distinguished translated children's book published in the preceding year" (Lynch-Brown & Tomlinson, 1998, p. 233). Written first in Danish by Glenn Ringtved (2016), the most recent Batchelder Award-winning book, *Cry, Heart, But Never Break*, personifies death as a friend, rather than a villain or foe as it might more likely be portrayed in children's books first published in the United States.

Other awards directly associated with ALA also draw attention to multicultural literature. For example, the Belpré Medal is awarded to writers and illustrators who best represent Latino culture in literature for children and youth while the Coretta Scott King Award recognizes books representing the African American culture (ALA, 2017). In the last couple of years, titles of books having been recognized in these areas include the following: *Juana and Lucas* by Juana Medina (2016), *Lowriders to the Center of the Earth* by Cathy Camper (2016), and *Trombone Shorty* by Bryan Collier (2015).

Other organizations affiliated with ALA also highlight award-winning multicultural books, including the American Indian Youth Literature Award, the Asian/Pacific American Award for Literature, and the Sydney Taylor Book Award, honoring the Jewish culture. Still another organization, the United States Board on Books for Young People (UBBY), releases a yearly Outstanding International Books (OIB) List in the *School Library Journal*, hence promoting and highlighting international children's literature.

Due to concentrated efforts of organizations like IBBY and the internet, the availability of international children's literature will continue to increase (Goldsmith & Diamant-Cohen, 2016; Tomlinson, 2002). However, it is likely that such efforts will be met with opposition.

While authors outside the United States may gravitate toward the topics of "alienation, living with disabilities, human sexuality, interracial marriage, and poverty" (Tomlinson, 1998, p. 5), audiences in the United States (and consequently teachers) may find these topics off-putting and avoid international children's literature that target, or even mention, these subjects (Zeece & Hayes, 2004). Still, other teachers may avoid international literature for fear that stories offering opportunities to reflect on social and cultural constructs may prevent students from enjoying it.

In fact, topics such as poverty, hunger, and genocide are more often skirted in US children's literature than in international children's books, or the topics are generally filtered through a Western lens (Joels, 1999; Thirumurthy, 2011; Tomlinson, 1998). Joels (1999) explains that international books, particularly the esteemed Batchelder books, deal with the messiness of real life by addressing controversial topics and offering insight into how people the world over deal with adversity. Tomlinson (1998), too, insists that topics found in international books accurately reflect the lives of both children living outside and *inside* the United States.

US children's literature, however, tends to take a softer, less direct approach than international children's literature. If not outright avoided, controversial topics are watered down and, as a result, books tend to gloss over or downplay difficult subjects.

A case in point is *A Birthday Cake for George Washington* (Ganeshram 2016), which depicts slavery as a somewhat pleasant experience, rather than exposing the horrors of those enslaved (Bowerman, 2016). In still another example, in *Henry's Freedom Box*, the illustrations (Levine, 2007) depict slavery amid images of slaves wearing clean and wrinkle-free garments in neat, if not pretty, settings. In fact, even while the protagonist experiences days in a small wooden box, the mention of muscle cramps, hunger, and thirst are avoided.

Intentionally or unintentionally, US publishers send the wrong message when they allow the misrepresentation of information and/or avoid controversial subjects because it is less palatable to people living in the Western part of the world. This message—that other perspectives or viewpoints are inferior or distasteful—is problematic if the ultimate goal is to prepare students to successfully navigate a global society (Thirumurthy, 2011; Tomlinson, 1998; Yokota, 2009). These distorted representations ultimately contribute to the reader's misreading and misinterpretations of the story they read.

Because book publishers are interested in appealing to the largest number of consumers possible and incurring additional costs for translating books and have they impact their profit margin, they tend to avoid publishing international books that address these touchy but critical issues. Lynch-Brown and Tomlinson (1998) warn that international books published in the United States may have been selected based on their lack of offensive material. For the most part, these books may lack important cultural elements and thus stifle their potential to foster cultural awareness.

NEED FOR MULTICULTURAL AND INTERNATIONAL CHILDREN'S LITERATURE

According to Levin (2007), US multicultural books skim the surface of other peoples, mainly centering on touristy type information. More pointedly, US children's books are often one-dimensional, focusing primarily on holiday celebrations, food, and clothing and ignoring the factors that dictate or influence others' customs. Unfortunately, in the United States, it seems to be the standard to which children's multicultural and international books are held. This standard, however, fails to provide an adequate foundation for students in this technological age (Dwyer, 2016).

Because of the progression of technology, teachers and students within the United States now have easier access to books about diverse people. Technology, including social media platforms such as Facebook and Twitter, also allow for the exchange of information with people whose perceptions and experiences may be far different from those encountered before.

These platforms also provide a way for people to share their concerns regarding the lack of diversity in published US children's literature. By way of illustration, in 2014, Ellen Oh tweeted the need to publish more books about and by minorities (Schoenberg, 2017). This response highlights the need for multicultural and international children's literature that provides students with opportunities to develop global awareness.

Unfortunately, even when teachers use multicultural or international literature with their students to address global issues, some teachers concede that openly addressing cultural differences or issues of diversity is frightening or disconcerting (Gay & Howard, 2000). In response to these teachers who question the legitimacy or practicality of having international books with controversial subjects in their classrooms, Leland et al. (2012) sagely argue that few pieces of children's literature are without conflict.

These same researchers also encourage educators to look beyond the accepted curriculum to identify books that represent diverse people and cultures. They even go as far as to commend educators for ignoring the status quo by taking risks and using globally themed books (Leland et al., 2012).

Whether we care to admit it or not, Diakiw (1990) suggests that children already grapple with tough issues—via television—and that teachers can provide a far better atmosphere in which to deal with unpleasant but relevant topics. Acknowledging the gravity of the situation, Leland et al. (2012) further state that "it takes more than a caring teacher and a good piece of literature to address issues of the developing world in classrooms" (p. 66). However, as they point out, the use of international literature in the classroom provides a solid starting place to foster an appreciation and awareness of others.

PRESERVICE TEACHERS AND THE NEED FOR INTERNATIONAL CHILDREN'S LITERATURE

Because no study was found that was solely based on the use of international children's literature by preservice teachers, providing the basis for this section of the chapter are studies that focus on preservice teachers and their use of multicultural literature or their use of both multicultural literature and international literature (Barksdale et al., 2002; Brinson, 2010). With these studies as a point of reference, it appears that, as a group, preservice teachers believe themselves to be ill-equipped to deal with diversity.

Therefore, by default, preservice teachers may avoid sharing multicultural or international books in the classroom (Barksdale et al., 2002). Remarkably, in one study preservice teachers were enrolled in children's literature courses, involving multicultural literature, but they were still unable to apply or even regurgitate the information that they supposedly learned in regard to multicultural children's books (Barksdale et al., 2002).

Similar results also were documented in a recent study when preservice teachers were specifically asked to identify books representing Asian Americans (Brinson, 2010). In fact, 100 percent of sixty-eight preservice teachers could not so much as identify a single book (Brinson, 2010) representing the shared culture of over fourteen million US citizens (Passel & Cohn, 2008). Interestingly, Asian Americans comprise one of the fastest-growing minorities in the United States (Cohn & Caumont, 2016).

Surprised at the finding that preservice teachers lacked specific knowledge about Asian cultures, we surveyed our own preservice teachers. We thought that we would encounter far different results for two basic reasons: (1) Asian Americans make up one of the three main minority groups in our area; (2) For the last twenty-plus years, a nearby Asian-owned manufacturing company has employed members of the community, including friends and relatives of our students.

Armed with this knowledge, we predicted that our preservice teachers would come up with titles for a couple of Asian multicultural children's picture books, like the *Name Jar* (Choi, 2001), *Suki's Kimono* (Uegaki, 2003), *Ruby's Wish* (Bridges, 2005), *Grandfather Tang's Story* (Tompert, 1997), or *The Empty Pot* (Demi, 1990). We were wrong. Not only were they not knowledgeable of children's books featuring Asian cultures, they were insistent that such books were seldom found in the elementary classrooms in which they studied and/or worked.

Upon further investigation, we discovered that while the number of published Asian international children's books has increased over the years, there are still relatively few. For example, while commendable, by 1998 UNESCO (United Nations Educational, Scientific, and Cultural Organization) had published only twenty children's books with an Asian influence (Tomlinson, 1998).

The 2017 list of Notable Social Studies Trade Books for Young People (NCSS, 2017) provides another example: In our analysis, only 7 of the 132 book descriptions prominently feature Asians. Applying simple economics may help clarify one of the reasons why Asian multicultural and international literature is a scare commodity. Even though it has increased over the last couple of decades, the demand in the United States is still small.

REASONS WHY PRESERVICE TEACHERS MAY AVOID USING MULTICULTURAL AND INTERNATIONAL CHILDREN'S LITERATURE

Lowery and Sabis-Burns (2007) make an important point that, before all else, teachers have to know about the availability of multicultural and/or international children's literature in order to address issues of diversity with their students. In light of this statement, O'Sullivan's (2004) revelation seems significant—that a large percentage of people who read translated texts are unaware that they are reading a books translated from another language.

However, in their earlier mentioned study with preservice teachers, Barksdale et al. (2002) dismiss the notion that simple exposure to international or multicultural literature is adequate in preparing preservice teachers to use multicultural and international children's books in their classrooms. While it may be anyone's guess as to why these specific preservice teachers did not retain information about multicultural literature, from research studies on learning we can assume that the learning was not meaningful, it was not internalized, and/or it did not connect well to their own schema (Vallon, 2014).

To more fully understand this conundrum, however, it is necessary to consider specific reasons as to why preservice teachers may perceive themselves to be ill-equipped to share children's multicultural and international literature in their classrooms and, thereby, address issues of diversity. First, a set of reasons may reside within the teacher candidates themselves. For example, preservice teachers may not recognize their own culture and, therefore, do not have a good basis on which to appreciate the culture of others.

According to Gay and Howard (2000), "Many European Americans claim they have no culture or ethnicity; they are simply 'Americans.' They assume that their norms, beliefs, and behaviors are universal givens, 'just the way things are.' This, of course, is not true" (p. 7).

Such a limited understanding of culture is not only sad but dangerous, especially because teachers have authority and influence over their students. By not acknowledging the importance of their own culture or being unaware of their own culture, they are likely to be blind to their own prejudices (Yokota, 2009).

With an indifferent attitude toward culture, preservice teachers may also be prone to ignore the nuances of other cultures, even when reading books that may offer opportunities to discuss cultural differences and similarities (Barksdale et al., 2002). Such incidences represent lost opportunities for both teachers and students. While teachers overlook the chance to model respect for other people and their cultures, students also lose opportunities to explore global issues.

Moreover, preservice teachers, who do not perceive their own biases, are unlikely to acknowledge biases at all (Colby & Lyon, 2004; Gay & Howard, 2000) because their own biases, although unrecognized, have already become the universal norm. Gay and Howard (2000) specifically point out that if this is the case, it will impede their ability to understand and address biases among their students.

Alarmingly, by failing to acknowledge prejudices within themselves and their classrooms, teachers could be demonstrating and perpetuating prejudicial opinions and behaviors. This insight alone is enough to warrant the purposeful use of multicultural and international children's literature in teacher education programs.

One other reason for the demonstrated lack of ability in handling issues of diversity via multicultural or international literature is that teachers are simply unaware that teaching about diversity is a vital classroom component

(Iwai, 2013). This lack of awareness among teachers and preservice teachers in the United States may be in part due to the fact that the majority of them are white females (Feistritzer, Griffin, & Linnajarvi, 2011).

This segment of the population, US females of the dominant culture, may have neither encountered nor purposefully considered the perspectives and challenges of people from other cultures (Colby & Lyon, 2004; Gay & Howard, 2000) simply because theirs are considered the norm. Unfortunately, the old-adage of "ignorance is bliss" is not applicable in this situation because a teacher's lack of cultural awareness can have an adverse impact on students' global awareness (Iwai, 2013).

Still another reason why preservice teachers may not be prepared to use multicultural and international children's literature in their classrooms is that they may be, consciously or unconsciously, resistant. Barksdale et al. (2002) approach this possibility in suggesting that preservice teachers come to teacher education programs with predetermined ideas about themselves, other people, and culture.

With this lens in place, if they are not offered opportunities to analyze their beliefs, they are less likely to embrace anything that they perceive as not fitting with their schema. While polemic, Gay and Howard (2000) go so far as to say that this resistance may have roots in "racial prejudices."

Undoubtedly, part of this internal conflict within some preservice teachers may also lie in their lack of exposure to other cultures and opportunities to converse or interact with people from other parts of the world (Barnes, 2006; Gay & Howard, 2000). Although in certain areas of the United States interactions with diverse cultures are limited or even nonexistent, the lack of exposure alone does not sufficiently explain preservice teachers' resistance. Something more internal seems to be preventing them from advocating for multicultural and international literature.

Gay and Howard (2000) use "fear" to explain these preservice teachers' resistance. Preservice teachers may be fearful that they will offend or provide inaccurate information regarding different cultures. In a related study, Lowery and Sabis-Burns (2007) found that more than 90 percent of preservice teachers indicated that they were ill at ease when addressing issues regarding ethnicity or race. It may be that this unease stems from a lack of knowledge or awareness about issues of diversity.

As the part of the dominant cultural group in the United States, some preservice teachers may feel that they do not necessarily need to know or be aware of other cultures. It seems that their unease is also a reflection of their fear of dealing with the unknown, which could possibly result in their losing power as the dominant group.

No matter the cause of this fear, Hunt and Hunt (2005) offer assurance for preservice teachers: teachers need not worry about being authorities on culture, but instead be purposeful in planning opportunities to share multicultural books with their students. They argue that the willingness to create a safe space for students to become aware of cultural and social constructs is more important than being a cultural expert.

While several reasons may account for preservice teachers' hesitancy or resistance to use multicultural and international children's literature, a second set of reasons target teacher education programs. Simply stated, in some cases, teacher education programs may fail to provide adequate training (Barksdale et al., 2002; Hadaway & Florez, 1990).

While they acknowledge that this situation can be an embarrassment to a well-established teacher program, Barksdale et al. (2002) insist that ignoring or turning a blind eye to the problem is unacceptable. They advocate that it is imperative to move beyond a state of bewilderment in order to address the fundamental issue of better preparing preservice teachers to use multicultural and international children's literature in their classrooms.

Notwithstanding, in today's given climate, educators have many obstacles to overcome. While not making excuses, they remind us of the many constraints that teachers deal with daily—overloaded curricula, tight schedules, lack of funding, strict state and federal guidelines, and an overabundance of testing requirements (Stallworth et al., 2006).

However, despite these obstacles, instructors in teacher education programs must be proactive in modeling the use of multicultural books to address diversity (Barnes, 2006). The potential consequence of not accepting this responsibility is sobering and long-lasting—a society ill-prepared to successfully interact with others whom they perceive as different from themselves.

NEED FOR A PLAN

As any effective teacher knows, a plan is essential in making certain that objectives are attainable. Therefore, if it is imperative that we foster awareness and appreciation for other cultures, the following three components are recommended:

1. Instructors in teacher education programs need to model by both identifying and using multicultural and international children's books. Their actions will then help ensure that their preservice teachers have the knowledge and skills to use this literature in their future classrooms (Barksdale et al., 2002).
2. While learning about multicultural and international children's literature, preservice teachers also need opportunities to examine their own biases regarding diversity as well as occasions to share and discuss these revelations (Barksdale et al., 2002; Barnes, 2006).

3. Teachers need to be purposeful in their intent to share multicultural and international children's books with their elementary students and make it a priority to engage their students in discussions about cultural issues (Iwai, 2013).

To help ensure the success of this three-pronged plan, Robinson (2013) suggests the following: Teachers must create safe environments in which students have opportunities to make connections from their knowledge about their own culture to the culture of others. Students also need to perceive this environment as a safe one in which to analyze information and freely express themselves. Without question, books that provide opportunities for children to consider others' perspectives, in addition to their own, are necessary constituents to the development of a safe and culturally aware classroom environment (Louie, 2006).

Simply placing multicultural and international children's books in the hands of preservice teachers only to have this literature overlooked on the shelves of classroom libraries is a shortsighted plan. Instead, Morgan and York (2009) caution that in order to reap the most benefits, we need instructors in teacher education programs to model reading multicultural and international literature and planning for its use with students.

Simply stated, multicultural and international children's books need to be read aloud and discussed in classrooms—at the preservice level as well as in elementary classrooms (Fisher, Flood, Lapp, & Frey, 2004; Morrison & Wlodarczyk, 2009). Because "teacher-led discussion is an essential tool in directly addressing stereotypes with multicultural picturebooks" (Brashears, 2012, p. 33) (as well as with international children's literature), time must be spent scaffolding preservice teachers in ways to use children's literature as a tool to encourage discourse about issues of diversity.

If we then embrace this sentiment as truth, as educators—preservice teachers, mentoring teachers, teacher educators—we need to accept the responsibility to move our charges, our students, beyond celebrating what people eat and wear to what they think and feel. While such topics may provide a starting point in bridging cultural understanding and clarifying misunderstanding, it is and should be just the beginning.

Some Western teachers, however, navigate toward superficial cultural topics and regulate cultural studies to only holidays and other special occasions. As a result, the chosen topics tend to be easy to address as well as noncontroversial. The Japanese practice of wearing kimonos, the use of different kinds of chopsticks by different Asian countries, and the different kinds of tea-serving rituals practiced by various Asian cultures fit well within these parameters.

Inasmuch, less critical thinking is required and controversial subjects such as governmental policies regarding educational practices and population control are easily avoided. By focusing only on superficial topics, the opportunities for cultural understanding are trivialized, marginalized, or stagnated at best.

If we are to promote true cultural understanding, preservice teachers need opportunities to discuss and explore pedagogical methods to use with multicultural and international literature (Pang, Colvin, Tran, & Barba, 1992). To be successful in this endeavor, such opportunities must become an integral part of the established curriculum (Hadjioannou & Hutchinson, 2014).

Thus, the practice of teachers using multicultural and international literature in their classrooms will hopefully result in safe environments for students to move beyond stereotypical thinking and to engage in deep conversations about relevant and important societal issues, controversial topics, and cultural differences. In stressing the important role that educators have in promoting cultural understanding, Barnes (2006) emphasizes that all teachers have the opportunity, if not the responsibility, to promote an understanding and appreciation of diversity.

CONCLUSION

In 1965, when cultural issues were moving to the forefront in the United States, Hutchins (1965) posed a question: "Are we educating our children for the wrong future?" Although he asked this question more than five decades ago, it is still relevant today and causes me to ponder the need to prepare our preservice teachers for a future that we know is coming and in some ways is already here—a future where diversity is the new norm and a global society is a reality.

With this understanding in mind, let's make *it* happen in the United States. Let's expect it, demand it, and support it—not only the publishing of multicultural children's books and more specifically international children's literature—but the sensitive use of these books in our classrooms. After all, we share the common goal of educating and preparing our students for the future—the right future—a future where the use of multicultural and international literature in our classrooms is no longer a surprising historical moment, but a valued and ongoing practice.

REFERENCES

American Library Association. (2014). Nation's libraries showcase multicultural resources as uptick in demand for multicultural children's books continues. Retrieved from http://www.ala.org/news/2014/04/dia2014prenglish.

American Library Association. (2017). Book and media awards. Retrieved from http://www.ala.org/alsc/awardsgrants/bookmedia.

Barksdale, M., Richards, J., Fisher, P., Wuthrick, M., Hammons, J., Grisham, D., & Richmond, H. (2002). Perceptions of preservice elementary teachers on multicultural issues. *Reading Horizons, 43*(1), 25–48.

Barnes, C. (2006). Preparing preservice teachers to teach in a culturally responsive way. *The Negro Educational Review, 57*(1–2), 85–100.

Bowerman, M. (2016, January 18). Scholastic pulls controversial George Washington slave book. *USA Today*. Retrieved from https://www.usatoday.com/story/money/nation-now/2016/01/18/scholastic-george-washington-slavery-book/78956160/.

Brashears, K. (2012). Appalachian picturebooks, read-alouds, and teacher-led discussion: Combating stereotypes associated with the Appalachian region. *Childhood Education, 88*(1), 30–35.

Brinson, S. (2010). Knowledge of multicultural literature among early childhood educators. *Multicultural Education, 19*(2), 30–33.

Cohn, D., & Caumont, A. (2016). 10 demographics trends that are shaping the U.S. and the world. Pew Research Center. http://www.pewresearch.org/fact-tank/2016/03/31/10-demographic-trends-that-are-shaping-the-u-s-and-the-world/.

Colby, S., & Lyon, A. (2004). Heightening awarness [*sic*] about the importance of using multicultural literature. *Multicultural Education, 11*(3), 24–28.

Diakiw, J. Y. (1990). Children's literature and global education: Understanding the developing world. *The Reading Teacher, 43*(1), 196–300.

Dwyer, B. (2016). Teaching and learning in the global village: Connect, create, collaborate, and communicate. *The Reading Teacher, 70*(1), 131–36.

Feistritzer, C. E., Griffin, S., & Linnajarvi, A. (2011). *Profile of teachers in the US, 2011* (pp. 9–14). Washington, DC: National Center for Education Information.

Fisher, D., Flood, J., Lapp, D., & Frey, N. (2004). Interactive read-alouds: Is there a common set of implementation practices? *The Reading Teacher, 58*(1), 8–17.

Gay, G., & Howard, T. C. (2000). Multicultural teacher education for the 21st century. *The Teacher Educator, 36*(1), 1–16.

Goldsmith, A., & Diamant-Cohen, B. (2016). Diversity through international youth literature. *Academic Journal, 14*(4), 38–40.

Hadaway, N., & Florez, V. (1990). Teaching multiethnic literature, promoting cultural pluralism. *The Dragon Lode, 8*(1), 7–13.

Hadjioannou, X., & Hutchinson, M. (2014). Fostering awareness through transmediation: Preparing re-service teachers for critical engagement with multicultural literature. *International Journal of Multicultural Education, 16*(1), 1–20.

Hunt, T., & Hunt, B. (2005). Learning by teaching multicultural literature. *The English Journal, 94*(3), 76–80.

Hutchins, R. M. (1965, September 11). Are we educating our children for the wrong future? *Saturday Review, 37*, 66–67.

Iwai, Y. (2013). Multicultural children's literature and teacher candidates' awareness and attitudes toward cultural diversity. *International Electronic Journal of Elementary Education, 5*(2), 185–98.

Joels, R. (1999). Weaving world understanding: The importance of translations in international children's literature. *Children's Literature in Education, 30*(1), 65–83.

Larrick, N. (1965). The all-white world of children's books. *Saturday Review, 48*(11), 63–65.

Leland, C., Lewison, M., & Harste, J. (2012). *Teaching children's literature: It's critical!* New York: Routledge.

Levin, F. (2007). Encouraging ethical respect through multicultural literature. *The Reading Teacher, 61*(1), 101–4.

Louie, B. (2006). Guiding principles for teaching multicultural literature. *The Reading Teacher, 59*(5), 438–48.

Lowery, R., & Sabis-Burns, D. (2007). From borders to bridges: Making cross-cultural connections through multicultural literature. *Multicultural Education, 14*(4), 50–54.

Lynch-Brown, C., & Tomlinson, C. (1998). Children's literature, past and present: Is there a future? *Peabody Journal of Education, 73*(3–4), 228–52.

Morgan, H., & York, K. (2009). Examining multiple perspectives with creative think-alouds. *The Reading Teacher, 63*(4), 307–11.

Morrison, V., & Wlodarczyk, L. (2009). Revisiting read-aloud: Instructional strategies that encourage students' engagement with texts. *The Reading Teacher, 63*(2), 110–18.

National Council for Social Studies (NCSS). (2017). 2017 notable social studies tradebooks for young people. Supplement in *Social Education, 81*(3), 2–16 insert.

O'Sullivan, E. (2004). Internationalism, the universal child and the world of children's literature. In P. Hunt (Ed.), *International companion encyclopedia of children's literature* (2nd ed., vol. 1) (pp. 13–26). New York: Routledge.

Pang, V., Colvin, C., Tran, M., & Barba, R. (1992). Beyond chopsticks and dragons: Selecting Asian-American literature for children. *The Reading Teacher, 46*(3), 216–24.

Passel, J., & Cohn, D. (2008). U.S. population projections: 2005–2050. *Pew Research Center.* Retrieved from http://www.pewsocialtrends.org/2008/02/11/us-population-projections-2005-2050/.

Robinson, J. (2013). Critical approaches to multicultural children's literature in the elementary classroom: Challenging pedagogies of silence. *New England Reading Association Journal, 48*(2), 43–51.

Rosenblatt, L. M. (1982). The literary transaction: Evocation and response. *Theory into practice, 21*(4), 268–77.

Schoenberg, N. (2017, January 4). We need diverse books: How social media gave wings to a grassroots literary movement. *Chicago Tribune.* Retrieved from http://www.chicagotribune.com/lifestyles/books/ct-flying-lessons-we-need-diverse-books-0108-20170104-story.html.

Stallworth, B., Gibbons, L., & Fauber, L. (2006). It's not on the list: An exploration of teachers' perspectives on using multicultural literature. *Journal of Adolescent and Adult Literacy, 49*(6), 478–89.

Thirumurthy, V. (2011). Building cultural bridges through international children's literature. *Childhood Education, 87*(2), 446–47.

Tomlinson, C. (2002). An overview of international children's literature. In S. Stan (Ed.), *The world through children's books* (pp. 3–26). Lanham, MD: Scarecrow Press.

———, (Ed.). (1998). *Children's books from other countries.* Lanham, MD: Scarecrow Press.

Vallon, A. B. (2014). Meaningful learning in practice. *Journal of Education and Human Development, 3*(4), 199–209.

Yokota, J. (2009). Learning through literature that offers diverse perspectives: Multicultural and international literature. In D. Wooten & B. Cullinan (Eds.), *Children's Literature in the Reading Program: An Invitation to Read* (pp. 66–73). Newark, DE: International Reading Association.

Zeece, P., & Hayes, N. (2004). Books for young children: International children's literature. *Early Childhood Education Journal, 32*(3), 191–97.

CHILDREN'S LITERATURE AND WEBSITES CITED

Bridges, S. Y. (2005). *Ruby's wish.* Illustrated by S. Blackall. Guilford, CT: Nutmeg Media.

Camper, C. (2016). *Lowriders to the center of the earth.* San Francisco: Chronicle Books.

Choi, Y. (2001). *The name jar.* New York: Knopf.

Collier, B. (2015). *Trombone shorty.* New York: Abrams Books for Young Readers.

Demi. (1990). *The empty pot.* New York: H. Holt.

Ganeshram, R. (2016). *A birthday cake for George Washington.* Illustrated by V. Brantley-Newman. New York: Scholastic Press.

International Board on Books for Young People (IBBY). (n.d.). What is IBBY. Retrieved from http://www.ibby.org/about/what-is-ibby/.

Levine, E. (2007). *Henry's freedom box: A true story from the underground railroad.* Illustrated by K. Nelson. New York: Scholastic Press.

Medina, J. (2016). *Juana and lucas.* Somerville, MA: Candlewick Publishing.

Ringtved, G. (2016). *Cry heart, but never break.* Illustrated by C. Pardi. New York: Enchanted Lion Books.

Tompert, A. (1997). *Grandfather Tang's story.* Illustrated by R. A. Parker. New York: Crown Publishers.

Uegaki, C. (2003). *Suki's kimono.* Illustrated by S. Jorisch. Toronto, ON: Kids Can Press.

United States Board on Books for Young Children (USBBY). (2017). USBBY outstanding international books (OIB) list. Retrieved from http://www.usbby.org/list_oibl.html.

Chapter 2

Authenticity

In the Eye of the Beholder?

Sharryn Larsen Walker

Within the field of children's literature much discussion has occurred about the authenticity of texts portraying diverse cultures, people, and views. This debate, which is rooted in the definitions of multicultural, global, and international literature, has most often centered on the insider/outsider perspective as it relates to the text, and it has implications for developing global literacy skills. This chapter presents issues related to determining authenticity and how to address it in the classroom.

WHAT DOES IT MEAN TO BE AUTHENTIC?

Mami's reaction to the reading of *Faithful Elephants* (Tsuchiya, 1997) in a children's literature course compared to those of her American peers illustrates different perspectives on the starvation of the elephants during World War II Japan (see Preface). Having heard this story as part of history and culture, many Japanese children understand the necessity of euthanizing the elephants as portrayed. The reactions of the American teacher candidates, rooted in their lack of knowledge of this World War II event, were as real and raw as Mami's. Both sets of readers' reactions were authentic, but can both sets of reactions be true? Who gets to make the decision about the authenticity of a text?

Singer (n.d.) labeled some Native American literature as "fakelore." He was not the first to challenge writers who do not possess an "insider's" view of a peoples' culture and way of life, thus objecting to the authenticity of the work. The discussion surrounding authenticity in the field of children's literature emerged from multicultural literature, and as it matured, the definition expanded to include global and international literature.

Yet authenticity in children's literature has been debated and remains a topic of controversy. For the most part, the discussion has focused on the writer's perspective of authenticity. The reader's reaction has not been as fully explored. To come to a deeper understanding of the controversy surrounding authenticity in this field, it is necessary to acknowledge several factors.

First, when determining the authenticity of children's literature, the importance of including books about diverse people and cultures in one's teaching must be addressed. Second, the definitions of multicultural, global, and international children's literature need to be differentiated. Those definitions then support the examination of authenticity within the field of children's literature. However, in this treatise the determination of authenticity is examined as an interplay between what the writer offers to the reader and the reader's power to interpret the work.

INCLUDING CHILDREN'S LITERATURE ABOUT DIVERSITY IN THE CLASSROOM

Through social media, students can connect with others from around the world in a matter of minutes. This informal and sometimes risky contact can shape students' perceptions of other cultures and people. To counter these interactions, teachers can expose students to world cultures by using children's literature in their teaching.

Reading children's literature that represents diverse world cultures and views helps students better understand themselves by identifying with the characters who may have the same life experiences, thus seeing themselves on the page of a book. Students scaffold this self-understanding by making comparisons between their lives and those from other parts of the world. In learning about people and cultures, students make connections and reduce negative stereotypes. Finally, using children's literature that represents diversity develops students' understanding of their place in a global society.

Dwyer (2016) promotes the creation of cultural understanding using global literature to develop global literacy, which the International Literacy Association (n.d.) defines as "the ability to identify, understand, interpret, create, compute, and communicate using visual, audible, and digital materials across disciplines and in any context" (para. 1). As the world becomes more intertwined economically, politically, socially, and culturally, the task of educating students about this connectivity falls to teachers.

Careful selection of books in which students can personally identify, make connections to world cultures and views, while promoting the tenets of global literacy is critical to a teacher's task. However, teachers must attend to the authenticity of the children's literature texts they use.

DEFINITIONS OF CHILDREN'S LITERATURE RELATED TO DIVERSITY

Children's literature has been used in classrooms to promote tolerance and learn about others (Short, Lynch-Brown, & Tomlinson, 2014). Teaching with children's literature is congruent with the National Association for Multicultural Education's (NAME) (n.d.) definition of multicultural teaching as it addresses the intersection of diverse cultural perspectives within curriculum and school life. In many American children's literature teacher education courses, emphasis is placed on the inclusion of multicultural literature, as it helps to promote culturally responsive teaching.

Multicultural literature has been defined as literature by and about marginalized groups within the United States (Short et al., 2014). Kass (n.d.) defines it as literature that addresses the many cultural groups in the United States and the world. Through consensus, Levinson (2005) developed a detailed definition of quality multicultural literature in which:

> the plot tells a fascinating story; the characters are believable and round; the setting enlarges the view of the reader; and the point of view reveals the inner world of each character; all the while demonstrating an awareness of multicultural elements such as age, class, disability, ethnicity, gender, race, religion, and sexual orientation. (p. 96)

Over time, the definition of multicultural children's literature broadened to include global and international perspectives. These terms have multiple definitions, thus adding to the interpretations of cultural perspectives. Short et al. (2014) describes global literature as books written and published in the United States, intended for US audiences, yet are set in another country. Books considered in this definition may have been written by immigrants, authors who have lived or worked abroad, who have written about family heritage, have researched a country and its situation, or have written in collaboration with another.

However, Lehman, Freeman, and Scharer (2010) refer to global literature as "books that are international either by topic or origin of publication or author" (p. 17) and focus on the diversity of people and situations outside of the United States. Hadaway's (2007) definition is similar in that it includes all types of books with diverse perspectives published within and outside the United States. Only Short et al.'s (2014) global literature definition espoused it as being American in origin.

Yokota and Teale (2017) distinctly define international literature as "books originally created and published in a country outside one's own and then made available through a publisher in one's country (and, if necessary, translated from the original language into the local language)" (p. 629).

Short et al. (2014) concur yet state that because these books were written and published outside the United States, the intended audience was for children from the country of origin. They further surmise that these books can be placed in three subcategories: encompassing books originally written in English and then distributed in the United States; books translated into English before distribution in the United States; and foreign language books, that is, books distributed in their language of origin.

Examining these definitions has implications for teaching. Multicultural literature focuses on the marginalized groups within the United States, and the availability of multicultural children's literature makes it conceivable that more of these books are already in US classrooms. Because the focus of multicultural literature stems from this perspective, the view of the world is limited. While it is important to provide students with opportunities to engage with multicultural literature, as they may encourage self-understanding and understanding of others, it does not present a global or international perspective necessary for developing global literacy.

Using global literature in teaching may possibly present a wider view of the world, but again because of the perspective of the writer, it may also present a Euro-American view. To develop a fuller understanding of global literacy, using international literature in teaching may be warranted but does present a challenge.

As Yokota and Teale (2017) acknowledge, there is a disproportionate number of US publications distributed to other countries than there are international books being dispersed stateside. The selection of international texts that fairly, accurately, and authentically represent the peoples and cultures of the time and place in the book is hindered by scarcity in the US market.

Making a distinction between the definitions of these types of children's literature when teaching can affect students' understanding of the world. Including children's literature that represents each of these perspectives is necessary so that misrepresentation of cultures does not become an issue. To encourage the development of global literacy, intentional teaching with global and international literature should include discussions about the authenticity of the text and the ways in which authenticity affects understanding of global perspectives.

DEFINING AUTHENTICITY

Defining authenticity is challenging at best. In its simplistic form, Merriam-Webster's Online Dictionary (n.d.) describes it as "worthy of acceptance or belief as conforming to or based on fact." However, when it comes to determining authenticity within the field of children's literature, much controversy has ensued about the "facts."

Fox and Short (2003) explore cultural authenticity in multicultural literature as one that diverges into a discussion of dichotomies, or of the insider/outsider view. Bishop (2003) defines authenticity as having to do with the cultural, physical, and social environments the authors of multicultural literature emphasized while honoring "authentic details" (p. 28), such as the accuracy of the information owned by the cultural group.

Short, Day, and Schroeder (2016) apply the principles of cultural authenticity in multicultural children's literature to their definitions of global and international literature. They contend that the books should espouse a worldview and share a factual depiction of everyday life of the represented group. Based on the previously presented definition of international literature, this could hold true. However, controversy lies in who is in the position to "judge" whether a text is authentic. The interplay between the text and the reader has long been acknowledged in the transactional reading process (Rosenblatt, 1978). But is enough credit given to that interplay when determining what is authentic?

PERSPECTIVES OF AUTHENTICITY

Although multiple perspectives on multicultural children's books were offered, Yoo-Lee, Fowler, Adkins, Kim, and Davis (2014) caution that only an insider to a culture can "sense if a book is authentic" (p. 342). They continue that no single perspective should be used when evaluating multicultural picture books with many of the previous presentations about authenticity resonating from the writer's stance. Woodson (2003) questions who has the right to tell her story, while Harris (2003) objects to European American authors who do not acknowledge their white privilege when writing outside their cultural group.

Noll (2003) argues that authors and illustrators have a social responsibility to accurately and authentically represent the culture of which they write, and Cai (2003) contend that the insider/outsider view is really a dichotomy between imagination and experience. Viewing books as "windows and mirrors" for children to not only view other cultures through a book but to also see themselves reflected in others is of importance when determining the authenticity of a children's book (Glazier & Seo, 2005).

There appear to be two questions centered around this portion of the debate. First, can the author, regardless of background of experience, write in a culturally authentic way if imagination and experience are used appropriately in the creation? If so, what is the reader's responsibility to the presentation of the text?

To lay the foundation of how to evaluate cultural authenticity, returning to the various definitions of multicultural, global, and international literature is warranted. As with Levinson's (2005) consensus definition of multicultural literature, Short et al.'s (2016) definitions of global and international literature influenced the criteria they established for cultural authenticity of international literature. They suggested first looking at the literary qualities of the work before examining other characteristics such as authorship, believability, and power relationships.

Additionally, Kwok (2016) states that the truthfulness of the translation should be contemplated when determining cultural authenticity. Regardless of the criteria and the cultural background used to validate cultural authenticity, the imagination, experience, and insider/outsider view determines what the author puts on the page as a presentation to the reader. Because of that stance, the creator of the text does have a perspective or bias based on personal criteria. Therefore, what is presented is subjective from the writer's point of view.

Although the writer has put pen to paper, believing what was written to be true from the personal perspective, the reader must still engage with the text. Rosenblatt (1978) posits that the reader was present in the reading engagement but was not given "center stage" (p. 4). About the same time, Bleich (1978) espoused that any reader should be allowed their own interpretation of a text, "as whatever one feels is right" (McGillis, 1981, p. 31).

These ideas of transactional theory in reading engagements, defined as "an active, fluid interchange of ideas . . . as between a reader and the text" (Harris & Hodges, 1995, p. 259) places importance on that interaction and emphasizes "each reader's subjectivity, albeit it with verification" (209). The reader often moves between what information the reader will carry away from the text to what experience is lived through the text (Probst, 1987). This is even more evident when examining the characteristics of text complexity, a process used to match readers to text (Fisher, Frey, & Lapp, 2012).

Examining text complexity involves three factors (Fisher et al., 2012). First, the reading level of the text needs to be determined. Next, the qualitative features, such as word and sentence structure, should be evaluated. Finally, the reader's tasks, including the reader's background and purpose for reading, need to be regarded when determining the appropriateness of the text for the reader. Teachers use the components of text complexity to match readers to texts, but left to their own devises, how do readers make decisions about the authenticity of the works they read? Can readers accurately evaluate authenticity if there is limited background with the culture or experience?

Short and Fox (2003) argue that the reader from the culture of a group needs to identify with the text as true, based on life experience, while those from outside the group need to identify and learn from what is presented. The stance of the reader, based on the reader's imagination, experience, and insider/outsider view, then becomes the foundation in the determination of the authenticity of any reading engagement.

An insider, who has imagination and experience with the culture, may make a judgment that the text rings true. However, one with an outsider view may discredit what was written for the opposite reason. The power of the interpretation lies with the reader, thus making the interpretation subjective.

AUTHENTICITY AS SUBJECTIVE

Subjectivity can be viewed as one's perceptions of beliefs or processes (Merriam-Webster's Online Dictionary, n.d.). If a writer presents his/her perspective within the text as true based on personal imagination, experience, and an insider view, the authenticity of the text is then subjective. At best, the writer can present the work from his/her perspective as what is believed to be true and hope that the reader accepts it as such.

Short et al. (2016) offers areas for the reader to deliberate when determining the authenticity of a text. Because value is placed on the reader's perspective and interpretation in transactional theory and text complexity, the power of interpretation is in the eye of the beholder. It is the reader who decides whether the text resonates, is believable, and connects to their imagination, experience, and view.

A reader's acceptance or rejection of the text can lead him/her to agree with the author, or make biased, misrepresented, and stereotyped interpretations. As with the writer's stance, the authenticity from the reader's perspective is subjective. In the end, it is up to the reader to make the interpretation from what is presented.

It is at this point where the teacher who presents multicultural, global, and/or international literature to the class needs to be mindful of the insider/outsider view. Not doing so can lead insiders to an insular view of their own perspective or lead outsiders to come to misrepresented interpretations. Although Soter (1997) stated that an informed reader may still reject the content of what was read, it is still incumbent upon the teacher to provide opportunities for readers to engage in literature that presents multiple perspectives. From those interactions, the reader, regardless of an insider or outsider view, can explore his/her own understandings of authenticity through verification of understandings, as Rosenblatt (1983) states.

The vignette of *Faithful Elephants* (Tsuchiya, 1997) in the Preface of this book illustrates the subjective authenticity from the insider/outsider view. Mami, who grew up hearing this story from an insider's reader view, understood the necessity of the starvation of the elephants. She felt the compassion necessary to relieve the elephants from their plight in war-devastated Japan. She verified her interpretation because the text resonated, was believable, and connected to her knowledge, imagination, and experience of her native Japan.

Conversely, her American peers rejected the content and offered other ways in which the elephants could or should have been euthanized (Amos & Finke, 2010). Their insider's view of their own culture prevented them from acknowledging their outsider's perspective of the gravity of the situation, and that starvation of the elephants was the best course of action. Although the text resonated and was believable to them, they lacked the ability to connect the knowledge, imagination, and experience of World War II Japan. Both interpretations could be viewed as authentic based on subjectivity; however, Mami's was supported with verification, while her American peers did not support their subjective interpretations.

As a follow-up to this experience, Amos and Finke (2015) conducted discussion groups with Mami's American teacher education peers. Through discussion, the teacher candidates deepened their knowledge, imagination, and experience of World War II Japan and the effect the story of the elephants had on Japanese culture. They also gained an understanding of how exploration of their subjective interpretation could affect their teaching. While the responsibility of determining the authenticity of the text still was held by the readers, it was the careful questioning by the professors that assisted them to move closer to subjective authenticity with verification.

RECOMMENDATIONS FOR DISCUSSING AUTHENTICITY IN CLASSROOMS

As teachers include children's literature about diverse perspectives in their teaching, examining the authenticity of the text should be part of the classroom discussions. The tenets of these discussions can develop global literacy, and in turn broaden students' understanding of the world's economic, social, political, and cultural connectivity. To guide the discussion about authenticity as a foundation for promoting global literacy, the following teaching tips are recommended.

- Include global and international literature in teaching and classroom libraries.

    As previously mentioned, it is conceivable that many US classrooms already have multicultural books in them. Therefore, it is necessary for teachers to increase the number of books that represent the global, but more

importantly the international, perspective in their classrooms. Titles of global and international children's books can be found at the United States Board on Books for Young People website; GoodReads; the International Digital Children's Library; or the Batchelder Award list.
- Use class discussions to differentiate between the definitions of global and international literature.

  When teachers use global and international books in their teaching, the discussions should include how the book fits the definition of either a global or international perspective. Doing so will aid in the discussion of the authenticity of the text. This discussion could center around studies of authors and illustrators of global and international books.

  Through these types of studies students can learn about the lives of authors and illustrators and how their experiences have influenced their work. Because many authors and illustrators host websites showcasing their publications, teachers can introduce students to the global or international stance of the books. Linda Sue Park and Taro Gomi are two who might be of interest when studying about authors and illustrators.
- Use close reading (Fisher et al., 2012) to discuss the writer's perspective of the books shared.

  Close reading requires students to examine the structure of one text, or a part thereof, through multiple readings with a different purpose for each reading. With each subsequent reading, teachers can focus the discussion about the writer's point of view, possibly including the ideas recommended by Short et al. (2016) and Kwok (2016); that is, examining the background of the author, the believability of the text, the power relationships evident in the story, and the truthfulness of the translation.

  Using these points in a close reading of *Words in the Dust*, a story of an Afghani teen by Trent Reedy (2011), could propel the discussion of how authenticity from a writer's perspective is subjective and in turn develop a deeper knowledge of global literacy.
- Use close reading and class discussions (Fisher et al., 2012) to discuss the reader's inside/outside perspective of the books shared.

  Finally, when using close reading and class discussions about the reader's subjective interpretation of the text, teachers can guide students to examine the purpose for reading the text, how the book resonates with them, the authorship and origin of the book, and the intended audience. To help students come to a deeper understanding about the text, the discussion should also include how an insider might view the book (Short et al., 2016).

  As Amos and Finke (2015) demonstrate in their conversations with American preservice teachers, subjectivity of the interpretation should also be emphasized. Selecting books from the Notable Books for a Global Society list would provide a multitude of global and international books from which to read with students. The discussions could also then expand to include the interconnectivity of the world economically, politically, socially, and culturally.

CONCLUSION

Socrates is credited with saying, "To find yourself, think for yourself." This quote is at the heart of the discussion about authenticity in children's literature about diverse perspectives. Teachers can develop students' global literacy processes by providing opportunities to engage with global and international children's literature.

These engagements should include discussions about the definitions of perspectives and how those perspectives affect the interpretation of the authenticity of the text from the writer's and reader's point of view. These discussions will help students see others through the window while reflecting upon their learning with a mirror. Doing so will assist them in learning to think for themselves while acknowledging that the interpretation of the text is in the eye of the beholder.

REFERENCES

Amos, Y. T., & Finke, J. A. (2015). Reading a different culture: The use of international children's literature in teacher education. In L. Nganga & J. Kambutu (Eds.), *Social justice education, globalization, and teacher education* (pp. 121–40). Charlotte, NC: Information Age Publishing.

Authenticity. (n.d.). In *Merriam-Webster's online dictionary* (11th ed.). Retrieved from https://www.merriam-webster.com/dictionary/authenticity.

Bishop, R. S. (2003). Reframing the debate about cultural authenticity. In D. L. Fox & K. G. Short (Eds.), *Stories matter* (pp. 25–37). Urbana, IL: National Council of the Teachers of English.

Bleich, D. (1978). *Subjective criticism.* Baltimore, MD: Johns Hopkins University Press.

Cai, M. (2003). Can we fly across cultural gaps on the wings of imagination? Ethnicity, experience, and cultural authenticity. In D. L. Fox & K. G. Short (Eds.), *Stories matter* (pp. 161–81). Urbana, IL: National Council of the Teachers of English.

Dwyer, B. (2016). Teaching and learning in the global village: Connect, create, collaborate, and communicate. *The Reading Teacher, 70*(1), 131–36.

Fisher, D., Frey, N., & Lapp, D. (2012). *Text complexity: Raising rigor in reading.* Newark, DE: International Reading Association.

Fox, D. L., & Short, K. G. (2003). *Stories matter: The complexity of cultural authenticity in children's literature.* Urbana, IL: National Council for the Teachers of English.

Glazier, J., & Seo, J. (2005). Multicultural literature and discussion as mirror and window? *Journal of Adolescent and Adult Literacy, 48*(8), 686–700.

Hadaway, N. (2007). Building bridges of understanding. In N. Hadaway & M. McKenna (Eds.), *Breaking boundaries with global literature* (pp. 1–6). Newark, DE: International Reading Association.

Harris, T. L., & Hodges, R. E. (Eds). (1995). *The literacy dictionary: The vocabulary of reading and writing*. Newark, DE: International Reading Association.

Harris, V. (2003). The complexity of debates about multicultural literature and cultural authenticity. In D. L. Fox & K. G. Short (Eds.), *Stories matter* (pp. 116–34). Urbana, IL: National Council of the Teachers of English.

International Literacy Association (ILA). (n.d.). "Why literacy?" Retrieved from www.literacyworldwide.org/why-literacy.

Kass, B. J. (n.d.). "Multicultural books bring the world to your child." Retrieved from http://theallianceforec.org/library.php?c=2&news=48.

Kwok, V. (2016). Faithfulness in translation of children's literature: *The Adventures of Huckleberry Finn* in Chinese. *Babel, 26*(2), 278–99.

Lehman, B., Freeman, E., & Scharer, P. (2010). *Reading globally, K–8: Connecting students to the world through literature*. Thousand Oaks, CA: Corwin.

Levinson, J. M. (2005). "To gain consensus on a definition of multicultural children's literature: A Delphi study." (Unpublished doctoral dissertation). University of Maryland, College Park. Retrieved from umi-umd-2710.pdf.

McGillis, P. (1981). Reader response: Literature and subjectivity. *Children's Literature Association Quarterly, 6*(1), 31–34.

National Association for Multicultural Education (NAME). (n.d.). "Definitions of multicultural education." Retrieved from http://www.nameorg.org/definitions_of_multicultural_e.php.

Noll, E. (2003). *Accuracy and authenticity in American Indian children's literature: The social responsibility of authors and illustrators*. In D. L. Fox & K. G. Short (Eds.), *Stories matter* (pp. 182–97). Urbana: National Council of the Teachers of English.

Probst, R. E. (1987). *Transactional theory in the teaching of literature*. Urbana, IL: ERIC Clearinghouse on Reading and Communication Skills. Retrieved from ERIC Database. (ED284274)

Rosenblatt, L. M. (1978). *The reader, the text, the poem: The transactional theory of the literary work*. Carbondale: Southern Illinois University Press.

———. (1983). *Literature as exploration* (4th ed.). New York: Modern Language Association.

Short, K. G., Day, D., & Schroder, J. (2016). *Teaching globally: Reading the world through literature*. Portland, ME: Stenhouse.

Short, K. G., & Fox, D. L. (2003). *The complexity of cultural authenticity in children's literature: Why the debate really matters*. In D. L. Fox & K. G. Short (Eds.), *Stories matter* (pp. 3–24). Urbana, IL: National Council of the Teachers of English.

Short, K. G., Lynch-Brown, C., & Tomlinson, C. M. (2014). *Essentials of children's literature*. Boston: Pearson.

Singer, E. A. (n.d.). "Fakelore, multiculturalism, and the ethics of children's literature." Retrieved: https://msu.edu/user/singere/fakelore.html.

Soter, A. O. (1997). *Reading literature of other cultures: Some issues in critical interpretation.* In T. Rogers & A. O. Soter (Eds.), *Reading across cultures: Teaching literature in a diverse society* (pp. 213–30). New York: Teachers College Press.

Subjectivity. (n.d.). In *Merriam-Webster's online dictionary* (11th ed.). Retrieved from https://www.merriam-webster.com/dictionary/subjectivity.

Woodson, J. (2003). *Who can tell my story?* In D. L. Fox & K. G. Short (Eds.), *Stories matter* (pp. 41–45). Urbana, IL: National Council of the Teachers of English.

Yokota, J., & Teale, W. (2017). Striving for international understanding through literature. *The Reading Teacher, 70*(5), 629–33.

Yoo-Lee, E., Fowler, L., Adkins, D., Kim, K., & Davis, H. N. (2014). Evaluating cultural authenticity in multicultural children's books: A collaborative analysis for diversity education. *Library Quarterly: Information, Community, Policy, 84*(3), 324–47.

CHILDREN'S LITERATURE AND WEBSITES CITED

Batchelder Award. http://www.ala.org/alsc/awardsgrants/bookmedia/batchelderaward.

GoodReads. http://www.goodreads.com/shelf/show/international-children-s-literature.

International Digital Children's Library. http://en.childrenslibrary.org/.

Linda Sue Park Official Website. http://www.lindasuepark.com/.

Notable Books for a Global Society. http://www.clrsig.org/nbgs.php.

Reedy, T. (2011). *Words in the dust.* New York: Arthur A. Levine Books.

Taro Gomi Official Website (in Japanese). http://www.gomitaro.com/.

Tsuchiya, Y. (1997). *Faithful elephants: A true story of animals, people, and war.* Illustrated by T. Lewin. Boston: Houghton Mifflin.

United States Board on Books for Young People. http://www.usbby.org/list_oibl.html.

Chapter 3

Cultural Differences, Interpretations, and Power

Yukari Takimoto Amos

International children's stories necessarily contain cultural differences. Children's stories from Asia, in particular, present significant cultural differences to Western readers because Asia and Africa face a higher likelihood of being perceived as culturally different by Westerners (Breuning, 2007). This could be due to more significant discrepancies in language, culture, and communication styles between most Asian and African countries and Western countries (Toyokawa & Toyokawa, 2002). The vast cultural differences, unfortunately, make the reader more vulnerable to misunderstandings and misinterpretations of the stories they read.

This chapter introduces theoretical concepts that explain the relationship between cultural differences, misinterpretations, and power. It attempts to analyze how and why misinterpretations occur.

ETHNOCENTRISM

In order to overcome cultural differences and understand other cultures from their points of view, it is important that we develop and strengthen cultural consciousness. Bennett (2014) defines *cultural consciousness* as the recognition or awareness on the part of an individual that he or she has a view of the world that is not universally shared and differs profoundly from that held by many members of different nations and ethnic groups. This definition proposes that an individual cognitively recognizes and acknowledges that others have different perspectives.

It is one thing to cognitively recognize and acknowledge cultural differences. It is another, however, to truly comprehend and accept those differences. For example, a global education advocate, Hanvey (1976), contended in the past that "such a fundamental acceptance seems to be resisted by powerful forces in the human psychosocial system" (p. 8).

In reality, the process of developing cultural consciousness is frequently blocked by ethnocentrism—broadly defined as "an interpretive framework based on the perception that one's own ethnic or cultural group (in-group) is superior to other groups (out-groups)" (Ragsdale, 2006, p. 204). This is a result of judging behaviors and beliefs of other cultures only in terms of what is normative and appropriate to one's own culture. When ethnocentrism exists, we perceive other cultures negatively, with such feelings as strange, bizarre, exotic, and unbelievable, while seeing our own culture positively.

In other words, it is not cultural differences themselves that create a problem. Rather, it is our unconscious or frequently conscious assigning of hierarchical value to such differences that creates a problem (Asante, 2003).

For example, Merriam-Webster's Online Dictionary (n.d.) defines a cartoon as "a preparatory design, drawing, or painting . . . a drawing intended as satire, caricature, or humor . . . a ludicrously simplistic, unrealistic, or one-dimensional portrayal or version . . . [or] an animated cartoon." This seemingly noncontroversial definition, however, is a great injustice to Japanese anime, which contains creative storytelling and demonstrates handmade artistic achievements (Price, 2001). Thus, the one-sided definition can be considered a manifestation of Western ethnocentrism.

Two other examples are school textbooks and children's literature. They are frequently seen as ethnocentric and lacking diversity. Racial and ethnic minority groups are often absent, although whites are always present. When minority groups appear, they are frequently portrayed in stereotypical and negative ways or remain in the background rather than playing a major role or being a main character. This representation naturally and unconsciously reinforces the idea that the majority white group is superior to other minority groups.

Ragsdale (2006) states that a key factor associated with ethnocentrism is "an inability among members of in-groups to acknowledge that cultural differences are not intrinsic markers of the social inferiority of others" (p. 206). We have a tendency to perceive even a slight cultural difference as inferior simply because it deviates from our own cultural norm, familiarity, and expectations, and thus stirs uncomfortable feelings. These uncomfortable feelings transform themselves into bizarre, weird, irritating, irrational, and frustrating feelings.

The uncomfortableness we experience because of cultural differences tremendously inconvenience us. Instead of trying to overcome the inconvenience, we tend to take an easier and more convenient way with less effort. As a result, the cultural differences are used to justify the inferiority of other cultures because if we believe that other cultures inconvenience us due to their inferiority, we can highlight our own superiority.

BELIEVABILITY

The imbalance between our capability to recognize and acknowledge cultural differences but our tendency not to comprehend and not to accept such differences suggests that it is difficult to obtain emic perspectives—out-groups' perspectives. When our awareness of cultural differences is superficial and limited to visible cultural traits, we may feel they are exotic and bizarre. We could be aware of both significant and subtle cultural differences, but when those differences contrast markedly with our own, we may feel frustrated and perceive the differences as irrational.

It is when we cognitively believe that the cultural differences presented in front of us are believable that we truly develop emic perspectives—how different cultures feel from their standpoints.

For example, while traveling in Japan, most Westerners find it odd and bizarre whenever they see adults reading cartoon books and magazines on a train. The aforementioned Merriam-Webster's Online Dictionary definition of cartoons necessarily nuances that cartoons symbolize immaturity; thus they are for children, not adults. Scenes of adults reading cartoons, therefore, register as unbelievable in the minds of Westerners, but in Japan cartoons are meant for every generation, from children to adults. A variety of genres of cartoons and their complex and complicated story lines make it possible for adults to read and enjoy them. In the Japanese viewpoint, cartoons are neither necessarily childish nor childlike. They are legitimate stories for adults.

According to Allport's (1979) contact theory, intergroup contact facilitates learning about the out-group, and this new out-group knowledge leads to prejudice reduction. Therefore, the best way for others to accept the cartoon culture in Japan and develop emic perspective is to have extensive contacts with Japanese people in Japan and gain knowledge about the Japanese cartoons through them. Since cognitive functioning involves knowledge (Bandura, 1989), acquiring and accumulating appropriate cultural knowledge about the out-group is essential for us to cognitively believe that adults' reading cartoons in Japan are indeed believable.

Unfortunately, acquiring adequate cultural knowledge is difficult in the current US education system where the curriculum itself is structured in a way that pays relatively little attention to countries, cultures, and people other than white Americans, and to a far lesser extent, white Europeans. Jennings (2006) further contends, "Americans, throughout their school years especially ... do not study about other people in the world, people whose beliefs, cultures, and status will directly impact their own lives in ways that were not even imagined a generation ago" (p. 2).

Poole and Russell's (2013) finding buttresses the point, as they found that younger teachers are not more globally aware than older and more experienced teachers. Since teachers play a crucial role in shaping students' academic experiences, it is essential that teacher educators, teachers, and teacher candidates all acquire significant knowledge about cultural others before developing cultural consciousness.

POWER TO INTERPRET CULTURAL OTHERS

Even when adequate cultural knowledge is acquired, however, such knowledge alone may not have a wide-reaching and sustainable impact on overcoming ethnocentrism and reaching the believability stage. This is because, according to Cushner (2009), schooling in general, and teacher education in particular, continues to address cultural learning purely from a cognitive orientation, such as reading, watching films, listening to speakers, and holding discussions around issues of cultural differences, rather than experiencing differences.

Reynolds (2015) contends that teachers and teacher educators who advocate for global education have experienced some degree of "border crossing" whether it be "having experienced some element of racial discrimination or by having been in an alternate culture for some time" (p. 32). Experiencing a loss of power due to not knowing the cultural norms associated with a new context (Merryfield, 2000) seems to be the direct cause of these transformed teachers' mindset. This is the main reason why teaching or studying abroad is highly encouraged in teacher education these days.

Experiencing the loss of power in a foreign country, however, could be difficult for certain groups, in particular the socially, culturally, linguistically, and racially privileged group in the United States—white Americans. The power the dominant group holds not only in the United States but also in the world makes it almost impossible for them to experience the loss of power even if the members of the group teach or study abroad.

For example, in our teacher education program, teacher candidates have an opportunity to teach English in Macau, China, and Honduras. Although these teacher candidates are immersed among cultural others in a foreign land, teaching English itself reinforces the power of the English dominance and its native speakers. When teacher candidates are not even encouraged to interact with the local population outside the classroom, nor required to learn the local languages and cultures of the countries where they teach English, conscious and unconscious feelings of superiority can easily be aggravated.

EUROPEAN AND AMERICAN IMPERIALISM

Power affects whether or not we can see cultural differences as believable or unbelievable. Due to the history of European and American colonization of the world, it is undeniable that Western countries hold the most dominant power in the current world, and such power is sustained by strategically excluding other viewpoints and ideas. The school curriculum in the United States is a good example. Since the curriculum itself is intentionally structured in a way that pays relatively little attention to countries, cultures, and people other than the United States, and to a much lesser extent, Europe, concepts, events, and situations are viewed primarily from the perspectives of white Americans, and white Europeans.

What is presented has become a norm, while what is excluded and why it is excluded have not been questioned simply because it is not present. Kim and Kim (2010) contend that white Protestant American ideals such as capitalism, competition, individualism, and independence are prized as the norm in school curriculum, but international issues and global perspectives are excluded, leaving students with the underlying message that the American way is the best and only way.

We had an opportunity to listen to a presentation about study abroad experiences in Cuba presented by undergraduate students. In the middle of the presentation, the audience was shown a series of classroom photos at a Cuban Catholic school. Among the several photos, a female presenter selected one particular photo in which desks and chairs were neatly arranged in several rows and columns, and stated with a concerned look, "In a classroom like this, there will be no collaboration among students. So, we modeled an American classroom so that pupils could move freely and interact with each other."

This female student did not justify why she felt that a classroom with neatly arranged desks and chairs will yield no collaboration among pupils. Rather, she treated her statement as something we all universally share and alluded that an American classroom setting will be more suitable for collaboration without even mentioning what that classroom looked like.

Obviously, the way the female student defined *collaboration* was different from the way Japanese people understood it. Students in Japan learn in a classroom, very similar in physical arrangement to the Cuban classroom. Yet there are lots of collaboration with classmates, even in a classroom with neatly arranged desks and chairs. Collaboration, in Japanese people's mind, does not necessarily require a great deal of space either, as most American visitors to Japanese classrooms are surprised at how noisy they are, and how much Japanese students talk!

What is most disappointing, however, is the fact that the white female student did not even consider that her idea of "collaboration" may not be the same in Cuba and imposed her idea on Cuban pupils as if it was something everybody in the world should follow. Her performance was a not-so-subtle example of American ethnocentrism, giving evidence that she had been well socialized in the tradition of American cultural imperialism in which Americans, whether consciously or not, believe that they can save the world by the imposition of their culture, thought, and traditions (Spring, 2016).

Of course, American ethnocentrism is one specific variety of imperial ethnocentrism, there being other varieties throughout history, practiced by powers such as the United Kingdom, France, the Netherlands, Spain, Japan, Russia, and China, for example, when they have dominated other nations. While it is important to have some understanding of the imperial ethnocentrism of other colonial and neocolonial powers, the task before us as educators in the United States is the urgent need to deal now with the destructiveness of American ethnocentrism on our students.

Ethnocentric Monoculturalism

The aforementioned example of Merriam-Webster's Online Dictionary with regard to its definition of cartoons is another good example of the social power Western societies hold to define sociocultural norms. More accurately speaking, it is a manifestation of ethnocentric monoculturalism. Ethnocentric monoculturalism is a combination of ethnocentrism (valuing of one's ethnic and cultural group over others) and monoculturalism (belief in one "right" culture) and posits the individual's culture as normal and valid, while other cultures are viewed as abnormal, inferior, or even pathological, and frequently this is followed by corresponding differential treatment.

Taylor (2006) explains below how one group's cultural values becomes the norm in a society:

> In the United States, the European American ethnic/cultural group holds the majority of social power and therefore determines the dominant cultural values. European American culture is considered the norm, and other cultures are considered deviant from the norm. When faced with the abnormal, many people react with distaste and want to remove the abnormal. (p. 203)

As Taylor's (2006) statement above indicates, a dominant group has the ability to define and impose its reality and beliefs upon another group (Sue, 2001). If one group feels superior to other cultural groups, it is a manifestation of ethnocentrism. However, if the group can designate their own cultural values as the norm in society, it is a manifestation of ethnocentric monoculturalism.

Sue (2004) lists five major attributes of ethnocentric monoculturalism: belief in superiority, chosenness, and entitlement; belief in the inferiority of other groups; the power to define reality; manifestation in institutions; and the invisible veil.

Because of the superior status normally assigned to the dominant group in society, the members of the dominant group are not only prone to "believing that their definitions of problems and solutions are the right ones" (Sue, 2004, p. 765) but also have a tendency not to be able to emphasize or understand the viewpoints or experiences of other individuals who are different from them (Eidelson & Eidelson, 2003). The members of the dominant group see any differences of other cultural groups as a sign of inferiority simply because they intrinsically believe in their superiority and their own cultural values have already become the norm in society.

In the United States, because of the power European American cultural groups hold to define social, economic, and political reality, its members have difficulty seeing "how the centric reality is a constructed, versus natural, phenomenon" (Taylor, 2006, p. 203). Because the cultural values of the dominant group overwhelmingly permeate in society's structures as the norms due to its dominance, it becomes difficult for the member of the dominant group to separate their cultural values from normalcy in institutions. This situation naturally makes the members of the dominant group unaware of the fact that the society's norms are actually a mere reflection of the dominant group's cultural values.

This is the way one group's cultural values become transparent and invisible. Invisibility is a product of cultural conditioning (Dovidio & Gaertner, 2000). Summarizing this process, Sue (2004) argues that people in the United States are trapped in a European American worldview that "only allows them to see the world from one perspective" (p. 762).

Whiteness

Ethnocentric monoculturalism is the invisible veil of a worldview that keeps the dominant group—European Americans—from recognizing the ethnocentric basis of their beliefs, values, and assumptions (Sue & Sue, 2003), and it is a basis of whiteness.

Beginning five hundred years ago, European invasions and colonialization of other lands produced ever-fluctuating and diverse social constructions of whiteness in European nations and their colonies. Whatever specific form the construction of whiteness took in an individual former European colony such as the United States, it legitimized a strong positive orientation to the white self and a strong negative orientation to the racial other. This white racial frame assumes that "whites are typically more American, moral, intelligent, rational, attractive, and/or hard-working than other racial groups" (Feagin, 2013, p. 94), and this becomes an integral component of the personalities the dominant group members unconsciously possess.

A strong ascription of superiority to the self naturally legitimizes ignorance about people and cultures that are defined as the racial other (Howard, 2006) because a sense of superiority justifies the attitude that there is nothing of significance to learn from people of color, either intellectually or personally (DiAngelo, 2006). This type of ignorance permeates in American education throughout K–16.

Whiteness exists only in relation to its differences—nonwhites—and functions as the unnamed, universal moral referent by which all others are evaluated, measured, and defined (Chubbuck, 2004; Frankenberg, 1993). Because of its assumed centered and superior location, whiteness devalues differences—nonwhites (Thompson, 2001) in relation to itself.

This elevating and devaluing phenomenon of whiteness in the K–16 context is critically presented by Kubota (2004). She reports that in the 1980s, most educational research conflated negative images of US classrooms with stereotypical images of East Asian classrooms, and that these research studies were influenced by the discourse of the US education crisis. On the contrary, positive images of US classrooms appear when the United States is sharply contrasted with and distant from Asian countries.

In this line of research, the negativity of US classrooms is associated with Asian classrooms, while positivity of US classrooms is intentionally detached from Asian classrooms. This juxtaposition ultimately highlights US classrooms' superiority, but rather discursively. In this case, whiteness's centered and superior location is strategically protected and secured by manipulating cultural others only.

Problems of Invisibility

The invisible nature of whiteness and its worldview—ethnocentric monoculturalism—presents significant problems when people from the dominant white group encounter cultural differences and cultural others. Simply said, we cannot even recognize something we do not see or are not aware of. Without cognitively recognizing that our viewpoints are not necessarily the right ones, and "our reality is only one of many others" (Sue, 2004, p. 767), the power of whiteness—making everything normal and universal according to white standards—prevails.

For example, we frequently hear the following comment from teacher candidates in our teacher education classes: "English is the most difficult language in the world. That's why English language learners have a hard time acquiring the English language." This comment obviously ignores the fact that linguistically speaking, all languages are equally difficult to master and there is no such a thing as "the most difficult language."

Furthermore, this erroneous assumption elevates the status of the English language and its native speakers because presumably, they speak the world's most difficult language with ease. It does not register with our teacher candidates who make this type of comment that they have self-confirmed their superiority over the native speakers of other languages because this particular reality has been normalized and thus is invisible to them.

Mami's classmates' harsh and negative reactions to a Japanese children's story, *Faithful Elephants*, as seen in the preface, are also a good example of the invisibility of power. As the members of the dominant group, these white teacher candidates manifested their power to define what children's stories should be like and determined that their interpretations were the right and only ones (for more detailed analysis, see chapter 6).

Within Asia, people throughout the region are profoundly influenced by the many varieties of Buddhism, Taoism, and Confucianism and the prevalent religions and philosophies. In Western nations and in the nations formerly colonialized by them, Christianity permeates the lives of many people, and knowledge of the numerous varieties of Christianity within those countries helps one understand their cultures, beliefs, and practices.

When Americans read *The Journey to the West*—one of the Asian classical canons—if they lack at least some knowledge of Buddhism, Taoism, Confucianism, and especially Chinese folk religion, they will be unable to comprehend the meaning of what they are reading. They will not understand the moral lessons that are an important part of each chapter, nor will they appreciate the fun, humor, and excitement that the novel conveys. Given at least some background in Chinese philosophy and religion in preparation, the reader's knowledge of Chinese folk culture and religious cosmology would, in fact, be increased simply by reading *The Journey to the West*, as the novel serves as an important text and basis for a significant portion of Chinese folk religion.

CONCLUSION: QUESTIONING AND REFLECTING ON OUR OWN INTERPRETATIONS

Diversity and inclusion have been increasingly seen as important and essential at the US K–12 schools where increasing numbers of students of color are enrolled. In teacher education, we attempt to diversify our curriculum by introducing multicultural children's literature and international children's literature. As a result, students K–12 have been more and more exposed to a variety of stories that portray diverse groups' histories, lives, and perspectives.

It is, however, not so much about the exposure itself that contributes to the students' development of cultural consciousness. Rather, it is more about how they accurately learn and cognitively accept cultural others' perspectives that could be vastly different, and sometimes widely conflicting with their own.

The cognitive acceptance of others' perspectives requires us to realize that "the knowledge base comes from only one perspective" (Sue, 2004, p. 767) and that important dimensions of human reality such as race, culture, ethnicity, gender, religion, sexual orientation, socioeconomic standing, and other sociodemographic variables unconsciously condition the ways we recognize, feel, and behave.

When exposing multicultural and international children's literature to K–12 students, our focus should be to help them investigate where their values and perspectives come from and how these values and perspectives are different from those of cultural others, and realize that their values and perspectives are only one of many. Without achieving this recognition, no matter how many multicultural and international stories the students read, their level of cultural consciousness will remain shallow.

REFERENCES

Allport, G. W. (1979). *The nature of prejudice* (20th anniversary ed.). Reading, MA: Addison-Wesley.

Asante, M. K. (2003). Education for liberation: On campus with a purpose. In V. L. Farmer (Ed.), *The Black student's guide to graduate and professional school success* (pp. 162–69). Westport, CT: Greenwood Press.

Bandura, A. (1989). Social cognitive theory. In R. Vasta (Ed.), *Annals of child development. Vol. 6. Six theories of child development* (pp. 1–60). Greenwich, CT: JAI Press.

Bennett, C. (2014). *Comprehensive multicultural education: Theory and practice* (8th ed.). Boston: Pearson/Allyn and Bacon.

Breuning, M. (2007). Undergraduate international students: A resource for the intercultural education of American peers? *College Student Journal, 41*(4), 1114–22.

Cartoon. (n.d.). In *Merriam-Webster's online dictionary* (11th ed.). Retrieved from https://www.merriam-webster.com/dictionary/cartoon.

Chubbuck, S. M. (2004). Whiteness enacted, whiteness disrupted: The complexity of personal congruence. *American Educational Research Journal, 41*(2), 301–33.

Cushner, K. (2009). The role of study abroad in preparing globally responsible teachers. In R. Lewin (ed.), *The handbook of practice and research in study abroad: Higher education and the quest for global citizenship* (pp. 151–69). New York: Routledge.

DiAngelo, R. J. (2006). The production of whiteness in education: Asian international students in a college classroom. *Teachers College Record, 108*(10), 1983–2000.

Dovidio, J. F., & Gaertner, S. L. (2000). Aversive racism and selective decisions: 1989 and 1999. *Psychological Science, 11*(4), 315–19.

Eidelson, R. J., & Eidelson, J. I. (2003). Dangerous ideas: Five beliefs that propel groups toward conflict. *American Psychologist, 58*(3), 182–92.

Feagin, J. R. (2013). *The white racial frame: Centuries of racial framing and counter-framing* (2nd ed.). New York: Routledge.

Frankenberg, R. (1993). *The social construction of whiteness: White women, race matters*. Minneapolis: The University of Minnesota Press.
Hanvey, R. G. (1976). *An attainable global perspective*. New York: American Forum for Global Education.
Howard, G. R. (2006). *We can't teach what we don't know: White teachers, multiracial schools* (2nd ed.). New York: Teachers College Press.
Jennings, C. (2006). Teacher education: Building a foundation for the global workforce. *AACTE Briefs*, April 24.
Kim, S., & Kim, R. H. (2010). Microaggressions experienced by international students attending U.S. institutions of higher education. In D. W. Sue (Ed.), *Microaggressions and marginality: Manifestation, dynamics, and impact* (pp. 171–91). Hoboken, NJ: John Wiley & Sons.
Kubota, R. (2004). Critical multiculturalism and second language education. In B. Norton & K. Toohey (Eds.), *Critical pedagogies and language learning* (pp. 30–52). Cambridge: Cambridge University Press.
Merryfield, M. (2000). Using electronic technologies to promote equity and cultural diversity in social studies and global education. *Theory and Research in Social Education, 28*(4), 502–26.
Poole, C., & Russell, W. (2013). Global perspectives of American elementary school teachers: A research study. *Journal of International Social Studies, 3*(2), 18–31.
Price, S, (2001). Cartoons from another planet: Japanese animation as cross-cultural communication. *Journal of American and Comparative Culture, 24*(1–2), 153–69.
Ragsdale, K. (2006). Ethnocentrism. In Y. Jackson (Ed.), *Encyclopedia of multicultural psychology* (pp. 204–6). Thousand Oaks, CA: Sage.
Reynolds, R. (2015). One size fits all?: Global education for different educational audiences. In R. Reynolds, D. Bradbery, J. Brown, K. Carroll, D. Donnelly, K. Ferguson-Patrick, and S. Macqueen (Eds.), *Contesting and constructing international perspectives in global education* (pp. 27–41). Rotterdam, The Netherlands: Sense Publishers.
Spring, J. (2016). *Deculturalization and the struggle for equality: A brief history of the education of dominated cultures in the United States* (revised ed.). New York: Routledge.
Sue, D. W. (2001). Multidimensional facets of cultural competence. *The Counseling Psychologist, 29*(6), 790–821.
———. (2004). Whiteness and ethnocentric monoculturalism: Making the "invisible" visible. *American Psychologist, 59*(8), 761–69.
Sue, D. W., & Sue, D. (2003). Counseling the culturally diverse: Theory and practice (4th ed.). New York: Wiley.
Taylor, J. F. (2006). Ethnocentric monoculturalism. In Y. Jackson (Ed.), *Encyclopedia of multicultural psychology* (pp. 203–4). Thousand Oaks, CA: Sage.
Thompson, A. (2001). *Summary of Whiteness theory*. Retrieved from http://www.pauahtun.org/Whiteness-Summary-1.html.
Toyokawa, T., & Toyokawa, N. (2002). Extracurricular activities and adjustment of Asian international students: A study of Japanese students. *International Journal of Intercultural Relations, 26*(4), 363–79.

Part II

(MIS)INTERPRETATIONS

Chapter 4

The Cultural Battle between East and West
Chinese Mulan *Meets Disney's* Mulan
Annie Yen Ning Yang

This chapter will analyze the differences and similarities in Disney's version of the *Mulan* story with two other English translations intended for young readers. The chapter argues that the English translations of *Mulan* along with Disney's adaption of the story have strayed from the original Chinese version that focuses on filial and patriotic responsibilities. Those filial and patriotic duties are in this case uniquely fulfilled by a woman instead of a man, who traditionally shoulders these responsibilities.

The changes made by Disney are alienating and confusing to a native person of Chinese culture. Disney's representation of *Mulan* would cause readers who are unfamiliar with the original intent of the story to miss important cultural lessons.

CHINESE *MULAN* AND DISNEY'S *MULAN*

Children growing up in regions rich with Chinese culture and tradition would be well aware of Mulan's legendary existence and the moral lessons one should take away from the story. *Mulan* exists for many in the form of a children's story, a simplified version in contrast to the historical and more complex version schoolchildren in China and Taiwan learn at a later age (Tian & Xiong, 2013). Although the character of Mulan's actual existence is debated and questioned by Chinese historians, the lessons from her story are unquestionably clear and etched in most children's minds and hearts.

Children learn that women can be as strong as men. They learn that family has profound importance in Chinese culture. Young girls learn that to be a good daughter is to do what is right for one's family. Children learn that family members help one another. They learn that collective interest matters more than individual desire. Finally, children learn to be attentive to their filial duties and patriotic responsibilities. Through the legend of *Mulan*, in both children's literature and textbook versions, values that are dear to Chinese people are transmitted. It is a tale both the old and young can recite with ease.

The tale took on a new look when it sailed across the Pacific Ocean and arrived at Disney Studios. It is not news that media industries borrow stories and cultural figures from other countries, and that foreign tales are modified into forms that are acceptable for Western corporate culture.

In his famous critique, the late Edward W. Said (1978) notes how Europe invented Orientalism in the late eighteenth century. Said analyzed how the concept was perpetuated by imperial powers such as Britain and France, and more recently by the United States.

In 1965, NBC created an Orientalized genie, from the story of Aladdin in the compilation of ancient and medieval Arabic, Greek, Indian, Jewish, Persian, and Turkish folktales and literature compiled in the text known as *One Thousand and One Nights*. Since then, such borrowing and adapting have more frequently made their way to the big screen and television. In 1992, Disney produced an animated version of the story of Aladdin; in 1995, it produced a corporate version of the Pocahontas story, stirring up both negative and positive sentiments in viewers.

Two years later, borrowing from Greek mythology, Disney-*Hercules* came to life; and the following year *Mulan*-Disney, vaguely based on the Chinese legend, was born. According to Box Office Mojo (2017), the film earned a domestic profit of about the $120 million and approximately $180 million internationally. Although it was not the corporation's greatest money earner, the film reinforced Disney's appetite for profit.

In contrast to much of the general viewing audience, academics were not thrilled with the content. Its depiction has been analyzed and criticized by scholars across disciplines. The main critique centers on cultural distortion (Yin, 2011). Yin (2011) argues that Disney's portrayal of Mulan has become the "normalized" version of a traditional Chinese figure. The Chinese figure Mulan is no longer recognizable to its people in its native land. The culturally cherished Mulan, with her traditional values and lessons, was reinvented by Disney, giving her new values, image, and associations familiar to American and European audiences.

Riding on a horse with a title reserved only for a Mongolian emperor and side-kicking with a character named after a Chinese pork dish, Disney has disfigured Mulan. Disney later published a children's written version of *Mulan* based on the movie, further disfiguring the legendary character from China. What is interesting and unsettling for a native Chinese person is the fact that both the movie and the book have strayed away from the main focus in the original *Mulan* tale.

CULTURAL APPROPRIATION

Cambridge Dictionary (2017) defines *cultural appropriation* as "the act of taking or using things from a culture that is not your own, especially without showing that you understand or respect this culture." The keyword in this definition is *respect*. Not all cultural appropriation is done in a morally questionable manner. Two major dimensions to determine the morality of cultural appropriation would be property right and identity attack (Young & Brunck, 2012).

Borrowing and taking cultural elements from another culture would not necessarily be considered morally inappropriate if it is supported by a genuine intention to share cultural knowledge. To change or modify the original cultural content only for profit distorts the cultural source and disrespects the people it was taken from.

For example, many people globally know of the traditional Chinese symbol of yin and yang. This symbol indicates the traditional Chinese value of balance. Artists have used the design to create jewelry and paintings. The intent is to showcase the aesthetics of the traditional Chinese symbol that communicates balance.

In contrast, Disney's animated character Maui, the demigod in the animated film *Moana*, upset many because tattoos have sacred meanings for the Maui people. Disney's misuse of them for commercial purposes demonstrates a lack of respect for the people who produce and value them (Tegeilolo & Rika, 2016).

Disney has been known as a storytelling organization (Boje, 1995). Its stories include not only domestically created figures like Mickey and Minnie Mouse but also tales from many cultures. If Disney had the intention of informing its audience of cultures from around the globe, not many would question the corporation's involvement in cultural appropriation.

However, Disney is in the business of making money, yet its profits have come at the expense of disfiguring and disrespecting many cultures around the planet. This has earned it a reputation as the public enemy of world cultures.

To demonstrate the gross distortion in the *Mulan*-Disney version, this chapter first summarizes the original version of *Mulan* known by native Chinese people. A comparison of the three versions translated in English is conducted on the following elements: time, Mulan's appearance, Mulan's family structure, her ethnicity, Mulan's fulfillment of her father's draft obligation, her horse, Mulan's sidekicks, her time in the military, Mulan's love interest, her accomplishments, and the story ending.

The three versions of *Mulan* are: Disney's book based on the hit movie *Mulan* and written by Cardona (2013); *The True Story of Mulan: Ancient China for Kids* by Donn (n.d.); and *The Ballad of Mulan* by Zhang (n.d.). The latter two versions are found online and targeted at children. The two stories are accompanied with illustrations similar to that in a children's book.

This chapter attempts to show the cultural distortion and lost cultural meanings through the comparison and contrast of the three translated versions. When viewing the culturally distorted and commercially produced content, one that sounds and looks nothing like the original version in Chinese children's literature and textbooks, one will understand the alienated sentiments felt by the Chinese when viewing *Mulan*-Disney.

SUMMARY OF THE ORIGINAL TALE

The original tale of *Mulan* was meant to inspire young women to fulfill their filial and patriotic responsibilities. The story is said to take place sometime before the Tang dynasty. But the exact era for the story remains open to interpretation. A young woman named Mulan felt worried because her father was being drafted to serve in the military. The military draft came during a chaotic time when the country faced foreign invasion from the Northern barbarians. Her worry stemmed from the fact that her father was too old and frail to fight. Her younger brother was too little to serve in her father's place.

Feeling responsible toward her father and country, she joined the army in place of her father. She shopped at the horse market for a horse and other necessities before joining the army. She spent more than ten years in the military fighting foreign invaders. She was careful not to reveal her true gender and fought numerous battles and gained many victories. The emperor wanted to award her with a high position in the government for her extraordinary bravery. She refused because she wanted to unite with her family and perform her filial duties to her parents. Although various versions of this basic plot emerged throughout time, adding elements as deemed essential, the basics stay the same.

STORYLINES DISTORTED

Time

"Thousands of years ago in ancient China . . . " starts Disney's book version. But the story, if real, might have taken place in the Han dynasty (206 BCE–220 AD) or Sui dynasty (581–618). The best estimate puts the story before the Tang dynasty (618–907), a little more than a thousand years ago.

Disney exaggerates the timeline of the story by stating that it took place "thousands of years ago" to create a dramatic sense of mysticism to the tale. The older the story, distant from modernity, thus, carries a certain allure for the audience.

Chinese civilization, based on written record, has been around continuously for roughly four thousand years. Disney's exaggerated time frame does not match authenticated history. Educated readers cannot help but wonder how could the tale of *Mulan* have existed before the existence of a complex civilization, developed enough for people to fight over territory.

Donn's version has a more ambiguous approach to time. The story starts: "Once upon a time, a long time ago, there lived a girl in ancient China." In Donn's translated version of *Mulan*, many details are intentionally deleted to allow the young readers to fill in the vacuum with their imagination. This version is somewhat closer to the original version known to many natives of China. Young readers would have a more realistic sense of Mulan's story, when it took place, and what really happened to her.

Zhang's version mentions that the story took place "long ago, in a village in northern China." The vague approach to time is strategic because the ambiguity allows the reader to situate this story in any time period. Without setting a story in any specific time frame, both the author and readers can exercise unrestrained imagination for the setting they desire this story to take place.

Mulan's Appearance

Interestingly, only Disney's version contains a description of Mulan's look. "There lived a beautiful young woman named Mulan" is how Disney describes her. In contrast to the original version, Mulan's look is not mentioned, and no other translations focus on her looking beautiful and young. This newly added emphasis seems to tailor to the Western audience that wants its heroine to be good-looking. But the fact of the matter is that Mulan's appearance has no bearing on her duties and accomplishments. In fact, the original version takes note on Mulan's attempt to be careful around her male soldiers to not reveal her femaleness.

The other two versions make no mention of Mulan's appearance in the beginning of the story. This approach seems consistent with the original version. Mulan's look is never a critical issue in the story. However, Donn's version describes Mulan's two colleagues coming for a visit and finding out her real identity as a woman based on her changed look, from a soldier's attire to a woman's. The vague description of the two colleagues' inability to identify Mulan when visiting her hints the change in her appearance from a man to a woman. But no detail is provided, giving the notion that her look is not central to the plot.

Zhang's version mentions her changed look toward the end. After Mulan came home from years of fighting, her sister "beautified her." That is another vague reference to her changed look, from a man back to a woman. Zhang describes Mulan brushing her hair and adoring it with a yellow flower. That is the closest Zhang comes to including Mulan's look in his version of the story. The purpose is not to highlight Mulan's beauty but rather to illustrate Mulan transforming from a disguised state to her natural and real self.

Family Members and Structures

The next distorted element is Mulan's family structure. In the original tale, Mulan has an older sister and a younger brother, along with her parents. Disney takes an interesting tactic in reconstructing Mulan's family. Disney reduces her family size and specifies her status as the only child. This status would contradict the reality and tradition of the time because families then preferred being big and were likely to have more than one child. There is no mention of a family dog or pet in the original version.

In the Disney version she instead gains a new family dog named Little Brother. A typical Chinese family at that time would not view a dog as a pet. Having a family pet tends to be part of the Euro-American lifestyle. The need for Disney to "Americanize" other cultures is perplexing and frequently revolting to people being portrayed in this manner.

In Donn's (n.d.) translation, the father is portrayed as a man thinking outside of the box for his generation and time. He thinks even women could learn. Thus, he teaches Mulan skills and she is able to take his place in the draft. This is an unlikely scenario given the cultural and historical background at the time. This is a highly Westernized version of how a father could be open to the opportunity of an unmarried daughter serving in the military together with men.

However, this same version stays true to the original tale in giving Mulan a brother who is too young to serve in the military. To ensure her frail, elderly father does not lose his life in battle, Mulan volunteers to take his place. Unlike the original version, Mulan bids her father farewell before joining the military and does not sneak into the army without his consent. Her mother and sister are missing in this version.

Zhang (n.d.) completes Mulan's family. Lines alluded to the father not having an elder son to fight suggests the possibility of a son too young to fight. As the story arrives at the end, Mulan's sister helps her to change back into a woman. When she goes to war, her parents are there to see her off. All members are included in this version, similar to the original story.

Mulan's Ethnicity

In the original version of the story, there is an implication that Mulan is not Chinese in origin. The line from the poem of *Mulan* is translated as "the Khan calls for many troops." *Khan* was used as an honorific title by the emperors of Mongolia. One famous figure is Genghis Khan, the Mongol emperor who conquered China and expanded his empire to Eastern Europe. This line from the poem of *Mulan* have had many researchers questioning Mulan's ethnicity.

Relevant to ethnicity is naming. Names offer insight to one's ethnicity in China, but of the versions mentioned none has touched on this issue. Disney renames Mulan in the military and calls her "Ping." In Chinese, Mulan's name, Hua Ping, can have several meanings. The term literally means a flower vase, but it could also be a slang term used to describe women with good looks but without substance.

Mulan Fulfilling Her Father's Draft Obligation

The three translated versions all divert away from the original tale of how the military draft is communicated to the people. The original version has the draft notice posted on a public board with draftees' names listed. Disney glosses over this detail by describing China at war, with each family having to obey the emperor's order to provide a male to serve as a solider. The draft is communicated by letter in Disney's version, instead of a public posting.

Disney also veers away from Chinese values in their depiction of the farewell scene. In the original version Mulan bids a formal farewell with her parents. Disney, with its emphasis on Mulan's imaginary, independent qualities, describes Mulan as putting on her father's soldier uniform and riding away without notifying her parents. Again, this act is much misaligned with traditional Chinese culture. A child who does not properly say farewell to her parents or other elderly people would be considered rude.

Donn (n.d.) describes the emperor's warriors coming to town to communicate the need for the draft to provide solider recruits. Like the original version, the warriors post a list of names of people who have been drafted. The story goes into detail on how the military does not take female soldiers. Mulan has to disguise herself to join the military in place of her father and leaves town disguised as a man with the other recruits.

While marching away, Mulan's father does not recognize his daughter among the warriors. This description seems to suggest that Mulan does not inform her father that she is taking his place in the military. Again, this is inconsistent with familial duty of obeying one's parents. Mulan going off to war without her parent's approval would contradict the traditional Chinese value of filial obedience.

Zhang (n.d.) describes Mulan as seeing the public poster of names of people drafted while shopping at the market. This is the closest to the original story. After gearing up, Mulan bids her parents farewell and heads to war. The emphasis on saying goodbye to her parents is more aligned with the traditional Chinese value of obeying parents. Mulan would not have gone off to war without informing her parents. Disobeying one's parents is a noticeable cultural taboo.

Mulan and Her Horse

A horse plays a major role in the story. In Disney's version, Mulan's horse is named Khan, and belongs to her father. The original version states that Mulan goes to the horse market to bargain for a horse for use in military service. Owning a horse would be beyond the means of most families throughout most of Chinese history. Disney elevates the socioeconomic status of Mulan's family, making them more prosperous than the original version, who were described as people of modest means.

The name of the horse is of great significance in Chinese history and cultural context. Khan is a title reserved for an emperor of Mongolian origin. No ordinary person could take on the title, let alone give it to a horse. Animals are considered to be lower than humans in traditional Chinese and Mongolian societies. For Disney to name the horse, an animal, with an honorific title only a Mongolian emperor should receive is degrading to the respected title. Further, it is another display of profound cultural ignorance and insensitivity surrounding Disney's production of *Mulan*.

Donn's (n.d.) version does not give Mulan's horse a name but describes how the family owns a horse and provides details for how the father has taught Mulan how to ride it. While it would be atypical for a Chinese father to teach his daughter horse-riding skills, it would not necessarily be so if Mulan and her family were not Han Chinese. Ethnic groups from Northern China were nomads who used horses and camels for transportation and food.

Again, that piece of information on Mulan's ethnicity is vague and still debated. No one knows the authenticity of Mulan's identity. Zhang's (n.d.) version is the closest to the original story. He describes Mulan going to the market to buy a horse to help her to serve in the military.

Mulan and Her Sidekicks

Further straying from the original tale is the addition of two mythical characters, a tiny dragon named Mushu summoned by her ancestor to help Mulan and a cricket named Cri-Kee. No other versions, translated or not, gives Mulan magical assistance from mythical creatures. This strange foreign inclusion into the story perhaps originates from Disney's commercial and critical success with the Jiminy Cricket character in the animated 1940 classic *Pinocchio*.

The original *Mulan* story focuses on human capability and endurance. Most Chinese probably feel it is absurd that Disney has included two anthropomorphic sidekicks—a cricket and a dragon—with the latter voiced and characterized by a famous African American actor. Such a portrayal might lead readers to perceive Mulan as being incapable of fighting as a soldier on her own, making it seem as though she needs magical assistance to fulfill her family honor.

As much as the Chinese love and honor their ancestors, in general they do not believe ancestors possess supernatural power that protects future generations. The versions by Donn (n.d.) and Zhang (n.d.) make no mention of any sidekicks, human or mythical.

Mulan in the Military

Chinese culture is a collectivistic one, with various levels, including family, clan, village, and nation. Disney emphasizes Mulan's desire to accomplish her goal and honor of her family but obscures the other levels of collective obligation that the Chinese must fulfill. The individualistic attitudes displayed by Mulan in the Disney version are more in line with Euro-American values, putting the self before the group.

Another area that most Chinese find foreign in the Disney version of *Mulan* is that with the help of her anthropomorphic sidekicks, she sends a fake letter to the general to convince him to attack the Huns, the enemy of the empire. Mulan's purpose for wanting this attack is for her to prove herself and bring honor to her family, which is another plotline that is not in accordance with traditional Chinese collectivistic values.

To create a fake letter is not honorable. For Mulan to want to bring honor to her family, she has committed a dishonorable act, in complete opposition to the cultural norms of the time. Disney's version of the story gets more bizarre, as the general follows the command of the fake letter and attacks the Huns.

Mulan is injured as a result of the attack of the Chinese army on the mountain held by the Huns. She is treated by the military medics, and her female identity is discovered. Chinese men do not leave women in danger, especially when they are injured, but in Disney's version the general and army abandon her. This makes no sense to a Chinese person.

In the original version, Mulan is said to take on extra caution not to reveal her identity, as lying to military leaders could be punishable by death. Donn's (n.d.) version describes Mulan as being careful in concealing her identity from the men in the military. After many battles and victories, the emperor wants to recognize Mulan and wants her to serve in his court. She refuses, citing her desire to be home with her family. Zhang (n.d.) takes the same approach in describing Mulan's military experience. Mulan is at war for more than ten years. During that time, she is careful about concealing her true identity. Both authors are keen cultural observers, realizing the importance of modesty and home for a woman during that time.

Zhang (n.d.) describes Mulan's military experiences extensively. He describes her as spending years fighting against the enemy, camping on the Black Mountain and by the Yellow River. It is not until after ten years of fierce fighting that she gets to return to her hometown. Again, this version is the closest to the original story by sharing similar details.

Mulan's Love Interest

The only version that offers Mulan a love interest is Disney's. No other version mentions a military captain named Li Shang who helps Mulan to grow in physical strength but leaves her in the mountains to fend for herself. The original version was never meant to be a love story for readers. It is more customary for the Chinese to advise soldiers not to think about family and life partners when fighting enemies. Disney's distorted focus on Mulan and her romantic love is in grave contradiction to the original purpose of the story that emphasizes bravery and valor.

Mulan's Accomplishments

It is unclear how much physical strength Mulan possessed in the different versions of her legend. However, Disney's version again showcases her individuality by suggesting that she has won the admiration of the military general by shooting an arrow into a tall pole. Again, the focus of a collective culture is to highlight the strength of the group, not the individual.

The emperor typically is protected by thousands of soldiers within the palace, but in Disney's version Shan Yu, the leader of the Huns, easily kidnaps the emperor and holds him captive. After she saves him, Disney has the emperor bow to Mulan, a female subject. There would be many ways to show gratitude, but a Chinese emperor bowing to a woman subject is not conceivable.

The only part in which Disney resembles Chinese versions of the story is the emperor offering Mulan a high position as an official. Mulan declines so she can return home and be with her family after years away.

The Ending

A single woman would never invite a single man to stay for dinner, at least not during the time when Mulan existed. It is baffling for Disney to have General Li Shang go to Mulan's house to bring her helmet, and for her to ask him to stay for dinner. If the asking was done, it would have been from Mulan's father. Mulan's behavior of asking a male, unknown to her family, to stay for dinner would be unheard of at the time. Such an act would have been perceived as behaving immodestly, dishonoring her family. Again, Disney's version demonstrates complete lack of knowledge of the cultural norms in China during that time.

Donn's (n.d.) ending is more similar to the original version. Mulan declines the emperor's offer to become a high official, and he sends her home with valuables. It is interesting to note that the emperor in this version offers her the gift of a horse. There is no mention as to what happened to the horse she brought to battle, the one her father owned in this version.

The act of the emperor giving Mulan a horse suggests that horses were considered gifts of great value, making it unlikely that an ordinary family like hers would own one. Thus, it makes little sense for Donn (n.d.) to write in his version of the story that Mulan's father taught her horse riding and that she rode the family horse into battle.

Zhang's (n.d.) story comes closest to the original version. It is also in the form of a poem, like the original version of the *Mulan* story. Mulan declines the emperor's offer to become a high official and returns home to her family.

One unique difference in Zhang's version is the description of Mulan's request for a gift of a camel. Camels are not used much by Han Chinese within the interior part of Chinese territory, but they are common in the periphery of the Chinese empire and used by national ethnic minorities in places like Northeast China (formerly known as Manchuria), Mongolia, and the ethnic Turkish populations in the far West of China, in what is now called Xinjiang.

Mulan's request of a gift of a camel to return home with alludes to the debate about her ethnicity, and whether the story arose as a tale created by the dominant Chinese ethnic group, the Han, or originated with one of the Chinese national minorities. Clearly, national minorities loyal to the Chinese emperor would have been the first to encounter and oppose the invasions of the Hun, or the Xiongnu, who were northern neighbors of China.

Consistent with Donn's (n.d.) and the original version, Mulan changes back into typical female attire with the help of her sister. When two comrades come to visit her on their way home, they cannot recognize Mulan. They are only convinced of Mulan's identity after conversing with her.

POWER TO APPROPRIATE AND ITS ADVERSE EFFECTS

After reviewing the three versions of Mulan's story and contrasting them to the original version, the two versions adapted by the two Chinese authors follow more closely to the original story. Disney's version has added elements that have disfigured *Mulan* and the intended purpose of the story.

Disney has distorted the time period and altered family structure and the family members in the story. They have ignored Chinese norms for behavior toward family members and made the characters in the story act like people from Euro-American cultures. Just as Jiminy Cricket aided Pinocchio in Disney's version of the story, Disney has invented anthropomorphic animal sidekicks to accompany Mulan to ensure that she has little creatures to assist her.

Disney has added a love interest to the story, but the lovers' behavior toward one another and Mulan's family is completely inappropriate from a Chinese perspective. The behavior of the Chinese emperor in honoring Mulan is so bizarre that it is difficult to contemplate.

The *Mulan* story and movie version created by Disney reinforces the myth that it's a small world after all. From this perspective culture does not matter. The Chinese are essentially Europeans and Americans with different types of clothing and houses. Disney's *Mulan* provides its readers with none of the morality and cultural understanding intended from the story.

To an unsuspecting audience, Mulan is like any other Disney female protagonist. She finds her path in life by struggling through obstacles put in front of her by evil people and eventually achieves success by marrying the right man. In the case of Mulan, the happy Disney ending puts her in a merry reunion with the handsome general who has fallen for her, despite the many conflicts and misunderstandings that occurred between them when they served together in the army.

To the natives of Chinese culture, confusion triumphs over comprehension when watching Mulan ride a horse disrespectfully called by the title of the highest Mongolian leader. Her consultant is a little dragon, Mushu, named after a famous Chinese pork dish. Worse, the cherished classic tale of a female warrior and hero has been transformed into a Disney fairytale about a young girl who defies all traditional Chinese values of modesty and collectivism and goes on a quest to find herself and love.

The disfigured Disney *Mulan* violently misrepresents the fictional character loved by Chinese and is an absurd parody of Chinese culture created to cater to common European and American biases and values.

The intent of this chapter is not to argue that all cultural borrowing is inherently negative. Historically, many cultures have borrowed from each other and modified them to fit into their own cultures. The Japanese language, for example, incorporated the Chinese characters into its writing system, and created two novel writing systems thoroughly based upon it. The practice of borrowing from other cultures and molding, to some extent, is natural considering humans' never-ending curiosity.

However, when cultural borrowing is done without paying respect to the culture of origin and done by those who hold power in the world, the practice of cultural borrowing is nothing but cultural stealing. Because of the dissemination power Disney enjoys worldwide, people all over the world believe that the disfigured *Mulan* and the distorted storylines are the ones that originate from China without realizing that the story they have read has little to do with Chinese cultures and people.

The characters, locations, and settings could be set in other cultures. However, the content of Disney's *Mulan* story has been accommodated to make European and American readers feel less uncomfortable and more familiar.

Children should be exposed to a wide variety of genres of stories from all over the world, including Asia. The ultimate purpose of such exposure is to introduce the concept of "respecting" other cultures that hold different values and perspectives and nurture the concept among them. Unfortunately, American and European children frequently read stories from other cultures that have been already appropriated to their own cultures. This basically reinforces the hegemony of Western cultural values and perspectives and thus does not allow children to acquire the knowledge that is necessary in order to gain respect for other cultures.

CONCLUSION

Chinese adults vividly remember the experience of being told and reading the story of *Mulan*. Chinese children learn of a woman who is brave and loyal to her family to a remarkable degree. Chinese children are inspired by her courage and willingness to sacrifice her life for her father. The lessons from the story are clear. One should fulfill one's filial duties toward parents and be loyal to one's nation.

With that learning in mind, Chinese feel disoriented when encountering Disney's *Mulan*. Disney's version is strange, unfamiliar, and insulting to people enculturated within Chinese culture.

REFERENCES

Boje, D. (1995). Stories of the storytelling organization: A postmodern analysis of Disney as "Tamara-Land." *Academy of Management Journal, 38*(4), 997–1035.

Box Office Mojo. (2017). Mulan. Retrieved from http://www.boxofficemojo.com/movies/?id=mulan.htm.

Cultural appropriation. (2017). In *Cambridge dictionary*. Retrieved from https://dictionary.cambridge.org/us/dictionary/english/cultural-appropriation.

Said, E. W. (1978). *Orientalism*. New York: Pantheon Books.

Tegeilolo, A., & Rika, T. (2016). How did Disney get Moana so right and Maui so wrong? Retrieved from http://www.bbc.com/news/world-europe-37430268.

Tian, C., & Xiong, C. (2013). A cultural analysis of Disney's *Mulan* with respect to translation. *Continuum: Journal of Media & Cultural Studies, 27*(6), 862–74.

Yin, J. (2011). Popular culture and public imaginary: Disney vs. Chinese stories of *Mulan*. *Journal of the European Institute for Communication and Culture, 18*(1), 53–74.

Young, A., & Brunk, C. (2012). *The ethics of cultural appropriation*. Malden, MA: Blackwell Publishing.

CHILDREN'S LITERATURE CITED

Cardona, J. (2013). *Mulan: Disney princess*. New York: Penguin Random House.

Donn, L. (n.d.). *The true story of Mulan: Ancient China for kids*. Retrieved from http://china.mrdonn.org/mulan.html.

Zhang, S. N. (n.d.) *The ballad of Mulan*. Retrieved from http://www.serflo1.com/Mulan.html.

Chapter 5

Remembering the Dark Past

Stories of the Korean War and Korean Immigration in American Children's Literature

Chong Eun Ahn

Modern educational settings strive to introduce children to intercultural encounters, often by having students read books containing diverse, multicultural, and international elements. Transnational or transregional migrations are part of the everyday lives of people in globalizing economies as well as the tragic wars of the twentieth century. Together, these migrations function as pull and push factors to make societies diverse and transformative.

In such a social context, educators and students inevitably engage in cultural differences in the classroom. Educators in the English-speaking world often use literature written in English by authors who represent their home countries' culture and history; some view this as a contribution to children's understanding of the cultural and historical backgrounds of immigrant classmates, their neighbors, or themselves.

However, the production of racial and ethnic hierarchies, stereotypes, and identity politics continues and develops in the classrooms and in other social spaces, even when encouraging cultural differences and historical understandings through the use of diverse materials. What could be the problems in using such materials? What could be more critical ways to use such literature of and by the Other?

While raising and responding to these questions, this chapter aims to provide methods for conducting historical analyses of minority children's books by focusing on the literature that presents the history of modern East Asia from Korean American voices. It analyzes how some Korean American authors of the children's books portray the experiences of Koreans in the mid-twentieth century, when people living in the Korean peninsula went through colonization, World War II, and the Cold War.

The analysis leads one to critically inquire about the (mis)representations of Korean history, culture, and identity in children's literature in English. Specifically, this chapter examines how memories of some Korean American authors function in the portrayal of Koreans in the twentieth century. As the stories and images from the selected children's books derive from the writers' or their acquaintances' memories of the past, a mixture of emotions and sentiments (e.g., sadness, fear, longing, warmness, love, and hope) appears in the literature.

The discussion herein argues that these perhaps nostalgic or perhaps historical elements ask for further analytical approaches to the style and content in the literature rather than simply taking away informative lessons from them. Simple knowledge-making possesses risks of children making not only ahistorical but also disempowering assumptions about the cultures and identities of various Koreans, Korean Americans, and themselves.

Celebrating differences by imagining that certain characteristics, sentiments, or stories from the books represent an authentic or legitimate Korean and Korean American past may limit children's ability to grasp that cultures and identities are fluid historical products that are changeable and challengeable (Kim, 1997; Yu, 2001).

BOOKS AND CONTEXTS

A gradual increase in Korean and Korean American children's literature has become evident as part of the rise of Asian American children's literature since the 1990s (Wee, Park, & Choi, 2015). The publication of picture books such as *Halmoni and the Picnic* (Choi, 1993) and *Dumpling Soup* (Rattigan, 1998) exposed children to Korean familial and eating customs. Korean folktales are being translated not only for academics interested in minority heritages but also for children in the forms of picture books and short novellas (Kim, 2004; Kim, 2008).

In the United States, the increasing Korean American population and the interests in minority education may have contributed to such an increase. While adopted Korean children may not be the targeted audience of these books, it is also notable that the adoption of children from Korea may have contributed to the increase. By 1995, approximately one hundred thousand Korean children had been adopted by American families following the Korean War (Oh, 2015).

These adopted Korean children and their American parents have shown interest in learning about Korean customs and cultures through culture camps and children's books (Yi, 2014). In general, children's books concerning Korean elements have become more visible to the American readers since the 1990s. General interest in Asian American literature often led to depictions of the noteworthy pasts of Koreans and Korean Americans in addition to their culture. Davis (2004) argues:

> Engagement with history become fertile ground for ethnic children's writers to (re)negotiate the varied and complex social and cultural history of their group's presence in the United States and the manner in which these groups have struggled to carve a place for themselves in American society and, importantly, in its representation of itself. (p. 392)

By the 1990s, literary works on Korean and Korean Americans' past and history had long been available to American readers. For example, Richard Kim's *Lost Names: Scenes from a Korean Boyhood* (1970), which narrates a Korean boy's experience with Japanese imperialism, World War II, and decolonization in Korea, has been widely assigned in secondary and higher education classrooms.

Like much of the minority children's literature echoing other tragic historical experiences of their ancestors, stories set in Japan's colonization of Korea and the Korean War became centers of some American children's literature as well. For example, Frances Park and Ginger Park's *My Freedom Trip* (1998) and Sook Nyul Choi's trilogy, *Year of Impossible Goodbyes* (1991), *Echoes of the White Giraffe* (1993), and *Gathering of Pearls* (1994), all depict the lives and experiences of people who lived on the Korean peninsula in the mid-twentieth century.

The main characters in these books, mostly children, present sad and difficult survival stories before they immigrated to the United States. This literature also represents larger historical contexts as the children in these stories narrate experiences of "enslavement" by Japanese imperialism, Russian communism, starvation, separation from family and friends during the wars, and lack of parental love, among other issues. In a way, these stories serve to teach about not only Korean history but also colonial East Asia, the Cold War, and cultural norms in Korea and the United States (Park, 2007).

Yet topics based on the past are subject to the changing sociopolitical contexts of the writers and their readers. As several contributors to the 1999 fall issue of *Education about Asia* emphasize, although *Lost Names* artfully narrates Korean experiences of Japanese colonialism, educators about Asia need to contextualize Richard Kim's positions as a Korean American intellectual and the influences of the "master" Korean narrative of colonial history in the book (Mastro, 1999; Minear, 1999; Wright, 1999).

In *Lost Names*, the main male character's depiction of the Japanese colonizers emphasizes their negative impacts on Koreans practicing Christianity and speaking their native language. Kim used scenes of students being summoned for wartime activities on Sundays and being beaten by teachers for speaking Korean or of their families being forced to change their Korean names to Japanese names to demonstrate this oppressive past. Many of these scenes are factual to many people who lived on the Korean peninsula under Japanese colonialism.

Yet there must be reasons why Kim's memories focused more on religion and education (Kim, 1970). The family Kim is describing in the stories is probably relatively rich and educated, and its members felt that they were losing their family heritage and religious freedom rather than suffering from starvation or the harsh exploitation of labor during the war.

Another question relates to how being a Christian Korean American during the Cold War influenced Kim's positive depictions of American missionaries and the severity of religious oppression under the Japanese empire. Basic questions in historical methods, such as the following, are crucial in analyzing literature that involves memory and history.

- Under what circumstances was the author writing?
- What does the author focus on or leave out? What do these choices tell us about the historical moment in which the author was operating?

Such questions are also essential in reading children's literature, as they contribute to strengthening children's knowledge and critical-thinking skills.

ANALYZING CHILDREN'S BOOKS ABOUT THE KOREAN AMERICAN PAST

Park and Park's (1998) picture book *My Freedom Trip*, for example, embeds such questions in historical methods. The first page of the book makes clear that the book covers factual and authentic experiences of Koreans during the Korean War:

> Many years ago, when I was a little schoolgirl in Korea, soldiers invaded my country. The soldiers drew a big line that divided Korea into two countries, North Korea and South Korea. In North Korea we could no longer speak our minds, or come and go as we pleased. We lost our freedom. Many of us secretly escaped to South Korea, the freedom land. This is my story. (Park & Park, 1998, p. 1)

Here, memory functions as a place where the past becomes alive. Although it is arguable that children do not need to learn the specifics of who the "soldiers" were or how and why the peninsula became divided, Park and Park (1998) vaguely present the why and how of the process of division as "the soldiers dividing Korea into two," which may be a critical question in the analysis.

This process not only involves complicated domestic factional politics in Korea enduring decolonization, but also—and more significantly—it explores how the global Cold War conflicts may have influenced the way Park and Park (1998) laid out the division so vaguely, lumping together the Korean, American, Chinese, and Soviet policymakers and military forces. The same reasoning applies to the pictures of a clear dichotomy: the dark and oppressive North versus the light and free South, even before the war.

This picture book is a story of fleeing, divided into fourteen chapters, that as a whole reflects the political rhetoric in which many Korean Americans during the Cold War were engaged. In the first chapter, "Peace," the main character, Soo, a schoolgirl living in the northern region of the peninsula, sees classmates disappearing from school in order to search for freedom land on a beautiful day. In the following three chapters, "Whispers," "Promise," and "Waiting," Soo's father leaves home to find the freedom land, promising that the family will get back together.

The remaining ten chapters show how Soo bravely follows a guide, Mr. Han, to leave her mother, flees the North, meets her father, and enters the freedom land, but never gets to reunite with her mother once the war breaks out. Thus, the book's story line is based on the pre–Korean War context, where the southern government is known for its authoritarian and corrupt control of the civil society, using anti-Communist propaganda and ignoring its share of responsibility in perpetuating the division (Cumings, 1981, 1997; Robinson, 2007).

Yet the experiences in the book vaguely, and perhaps intentionally, lead to the imagination of the South as the freedom land. The frequent appearance of the term *freedom land* not only presents an ahistorical picture of the Korean peninsula in the mid to late 1940s but also engraves a black-and-white image of each government. In the penultimate chapter, "Freedom," a North Korean soldier who caught Soo and her guide Mr. Han releases Soo. Then the following scene appears:

> Mr. Han guided me toward a dark, mossy opening in the woods. "I must go back, but you are free, Soo. Go Go!" I ran without thinking. I was so frightened I forgot where I was going. Then I saw the river. The water was so blue, my eyes were swimming in every direction! And there was my father, waving wildly from the other side. The freedom land! "Soo! Soo!" he cried out. "*Apa!*" I cried back. I rushed into the river, embracing the sun and the sky. (Park & Park, 1998, p. 27)

The river-crossing scene actualizes liberation. Across the river is where the sun and the sky greet you. It is a place where one in actuality becomes free.

But readers need to ask the following questions to engage in critical learning:

- Liberation from what exactly? How?
- Why and how is there a land of (ultimate) freedom?

While these questions may be difficult for children in preK–9 to raise, educators can lead students to question why freedom matters to Soo and the author so much, what Soo (or the author) means by freedom, and what is missing in the depiction of the freedom land. Discussions of these questions will lead students to think further about the background of the author and history making in the book.

More explicit discussions about authors' positions as minority Americans would also be helpful. In addition to the questions concerning the authors' ideological or political assumptions about the dark, oppressive North regime versus the bright, liberating South, the expression of freedom serves as a lingering representation of Korean Americans able to continue their migration from South Korea to the United States. Resolution and bravery lie at the heart of the continuing processes of migration and liberation. The final page in the book, which serves as an epilogue, states the following:

> Many years have passed. I am no longer a little schoolgirl. But I still think about Mr. Han, my gentle guide, and about the soldier who set me free. Mostly, I think about my mother. When the evening is full of moon and warm winds, I can still hear her cry—Be brave, Soo! Brave for the rest of my life. (Park & Park, 1998, p. 30)

Sadness due to the girl's permanent separation from her mother continues, yet it contrastingly empowers her message to be brave, which is at the core of Soo's life even after the liberation. Soo's memory emphasizes the shared experiences of Koreans who suffer from the division, especially separation from family members, and who are brave, as they have successfully found freedom despite difficulties.

In Choi's trilogy, Korean Americans are also represented as determined and strong-willed survivors of a dark past. The first book in the series, *Year of Impossible Goodbyes* (1991), traces the sad and dark history of Koreans before the liberation from Japan, meaning migration to the southern regime before the war. The main character, the young girl Sookan, and her family's struggles tell the story of the Japanese colonial occupation and postcolonial liberation in ten chapters.

The sequel *Echoes of the White Giraffe* (1993) discusses Sookan's struggles in her youth during the Korean War (1950–1953). The final book, *Gathering of Pearls* (1994), depicts Sookan's encounters with a new culture and society as she moves to the United States to attend college (1954 onward). The following discussion focuses on the story told in the first book.

As a fictional story for children, rather than a picture book, *Year of Impossible Goodbyes* details the experiences of Koreans in the North since the Japanese occupation. Sookan's family makes a living by running a sock factory that provides socks for the Japanese Imperial Army during World War II. The family is separated as members are sent to labor camps, move to Manchuria for the Korean independence movement, and live at a Catholic covenant.

The remaining members in the house experience the harshness of Japanese police, who visit the house frequently to check the factory's productivity. Sookan says goodbye to her grandfather for good as the result of a police visit to the house during an episode of bad timing. She witnesses teenage female laborers in the factory being sent to the military services (probably forced to render sexual services to the armed forces in wartime Japan in "comfort stations").

She experiences the maltreatment of Korean students at school by a Japanese teacher, and experiences growing hunger until the end of the war. Overall, the story presents Sookan's experiences under Japanese colonialism as grim and bleak. Yet the end of the war, which occurs in chapter 6, was not the end of the dark period. The country's division (the implementation of Soviet control in North Korea) is the main theme in the latter part of the book.

Similar to Park and Park's (1998) emphasis on the oppressive nature of the Communist regime, Sookan's uncomfortable feelings about and pressures from the Communist government become clear:

> I found it harder and harder to tolerate the Korean women who worked so hard for the Party, fervently spreading Communist philosophy. They were so happy and proud to be leaders, and we called them our Town Reds. I was tired of it all, but there was no choice. We had to go to work and to the Party meetings every day to have our red I.D. books stamped. Each week, they counted the stamps before they gave us our rice ration.... A little boy named Hansin was so thrilled to be a little proletarian that he talked all the time. One day he mentioned that a stranger had come to his house, and after that we never saw him or his family again. I started to grow more and more afraid of the Russians and the Town Reds. (Choi & Choi, 1991, pp. 110–11)

As these stories attest, most of the experiences during the Soviet control of North Korea appear politically and socially overbearing to Sookan—and probably to the readers as well.

Similar to Soo's search for freedom in *My Freedom Trip*, Sookan, her brother, and their mother attempt to leave North Korea with the help of a former sock factory employee and their aunt. They hear that their other siblings and father are settled in South Korea and decide to follow a guide to escape the grim regime.

On the way south, the siblings are separated from their mother, as their guide is a fraud. They search for their mother while begging for food. With the help of a railroad station employee, the children reach South Korea. The family is united at the end, as Soo's mother also escapes from forced labor as a housemaid for a Russian officer. The epilogue implies that another difficult period, the Korean War (1950–1953), awaits them. The family's reunion and hope for the future, however, are evident as Sookan and her brother are in the safer and freer southern society.

Overall, *Year of Impossible Goodbyes* throws out a similar message as *My Freedom Trip*: the resilient struggle to liberate oneself from dark regimes. Detailed information, such as daily forced labor, revolutionary activism in the neighborhood, and reverence for Mother Russia in Choi's book, allows readers to draw clearer pictures about the Communist regime. However, this specific narrative also requires critical analysis:

> I began to follow the jeep with the others, but Mother grabbed me by the arm. "You are not going anywhere," she told me. "We are waiting right here until your father and brothers come. Then we are going south to where the Americans are." (Choi & Choi, 1991, p. 104)

This scene occurs when the Soviet army enters Pyongyang to liberate Koreans from the Japanese empire.

Even at that moment, Sookan's mother knows that this could mean danger and that they need to move south, where the Americans are. As Elaine H. Kim argues, "America is seen as a promise or a promised land. Sookan imagines America vaguely is the place where she will no longer feel empty, restless, and incomplete" (1997, p. 167). Using this scene, the following questions would be helpful in building critical analysis skills for students in the classroom.

- What images does Sookan have about America and the Soviet Union? Why does Sookan's mother prefer American control before she experiences Soviet control? Does this have anything to do with her position as a Christian woman influenced by American missionaries? Why or why not?
- What might her social and political position be that influences her to be cautious about the Russians and/or the Communists?
- Is the author expressing her perspectives on Russians and Communists in these scenes? Why or why not?

Although historical facts, such as how oppressive the Russian Communist regime was to the ordinary people of North Korea in the 1940s, may be debatable at the academic level, questioning the positions of the author shown in the book would engage children in practicing critical analysis.

More simply, children can question why and how the mother knows that the family should move to the American regime to the south even before experiencing the division. They can then extend their curiosity to speculate about larger historical contexts. Choi's depiction of Russians and Russian communism as the major oppressor in North Korea possibly comes from the Cold War rhetoric to which Choi was exposed as a Korean American from the 1950s to 1980s, rather than her vivid memory of the Russians or historical research on the Soviet Union in North Korea.

Taking fictional stories as historical facts becomes problematic as the reading guides and reviews of Choi's works emphasize Choi's biography. Unlike Park and Park's (1998) introductory passage, Choi does not make such an introduction or authenticate the stories by explicitly exposing the narrator's (and the author's) identity in her story. Yet the covers and back pages of the trilogy introduce reviews that identified her first book as an authentic story with educational and historical messages (Choi, 1994).

Multiple reading guide sources (e.g., Scanlon, 2000) also categorize Choi's trilogy as autobiographical fiction or fictionalized autobiography by introducing Choi's biography as follows:

> Sook Nyul Choi was born in 1937 in Pyongyang in what is now North Korea. Like the young character in her novel, Choi fled the hardships of the Communist takeover of North Korea by escaping to South Korea when she was a young girl. When Choi was twenty-one, she emigrated to the United States, where she then attended Manhattan College, in New York. . . . Since all of Choi's novels are based on her personal experience, her books can be read as a journey through her life. (Constantakis, 2009, p. 313)

Like Constantakis (2009), Day (1994) also introduces Choi's experiences in the Korean peninsula and stories of immigration to the United States, categorizing her works as "fictionalized autobiography" or "autobiography" (pp. 49–51). Such guides strongly authenticate Choi's trilogy as a historical record of the Korean past, not as the memory of a Korean American. What these guides and reviews suggest as assignments or classroom activities may be helpful in diversifying children's knowledge about minority past while also broadening their imaginative scopes.

As Day (1994) proposes, students can learn these lessons by pondering questions, such as "What did Choi's family do when they were free? What happened to end this freedom?" (p. 52) or responding to prompts, such as "Make a list of the cruelties suffered by Choi's family and neighbors. Discuss how they coped with each of these problems. What advice do you think Sookan might have for other refugees?" (p. 50). Children will be able to collect more data regarding immigrants' past experiences and migration processes.

Stories of the resilient struggles of immigrants in their youth can also lead children to think about moralized concepts, such as bravery, willfulness, honesty, and filial relationships, as sources of empowerment in the students' daily lives. What could benefit children in strengthening their analytical and critical-thinking skills, however, would be questions that stir up the believed authenticity of the representations of the past. Questions about the author's position, source, and narrative style can lead children to understand that history is not simply about facts but also involves making one's arguments and positions.

CONCLUSION

This chapter's brief analysis and questions share other disciplinary concerns. Literary scholars have made critical interventions helpful in supporting this chapter's position. Elaine Kim (1997) notes that "many Korean-American viewpoints are represented only through the filtering memories of an English-speaking descendent or the modifying lens of a writer's class privilege. The voices of the 'mainstream' or majority of Korean Americans have thus been faint and mediated" (p. 156).

Kim criticizes that the experiences of relatively lower-class immigrants are almost entirely missing in Korean American literature. Sung (2009) analyzed book reviews and annotations of Korean American picture books and argues that the emphasis on the long-distance travel from Korea to the United States "enhances the connotations of a 'far-away' exotic country" and "guessing national identity with names" (pp. 235–37). A point more related to this chapter is Sung's (2009) note that "the simplicity of book information in these annotations perpetuates binary mindsets in which the negative (Korea) is solved (U.S.)" (p. 238).

Examining Korean American authors' contrasts between a sad past and possibly better today, this chapter emphasizes that there are multiple risks in using these literary stories, especially the sad stories of minorities, in children's literature. These stories may lead children to sympathize with people from different times and regions, which can be helpful in building moral sensibilities.

Yet such an approach does not necessarily educate children about the historical processes that caused such dire situations for immigrants or foreigners. It does not engage children in critical conversations about the global society they are living in today. It can make strong impressions that these minorities are from perpetually dark places, where individual and social successes are not possible. Koreans within the peninsula, for clear example, remain fixed as a group still suffering from the problems of division to this day.

Korean Americans, on the other hand, are represented as courageous people who overcame such problems. It creates not only misunderstandings but also stereotypes about immigrants and foreigners, their cultures, and histories.

More importantly, such an approach allows readers, especially children, to position themselves in a simplistically relative spectrum of oppression in contrast to freedom. In this case of Korean American stories of liberation from colonialism and communism in their journeys to the United States, children may imagine a dichotomized picture of the Americans as the emancipators versus the Korean immigrants as the rescued.

The uncritical approach makes a strong impression that America is the place of emancipation and freedom. It dismisses the various oppressive circumstances Korean immigrants had to struggle with as labor migrants, small business owners, or military brides in the United States (Kim, 1997). It also ahistorically embellishes the majority of immigrants' searches for security from immediate political and social exigencies (Yuh, 2005).

Only historical analysis of these literary works as both primary and secondary sources can help students challenge and avoid such misunderstandings. Literary works should not be simply considered as authentic representations of the Others' past. In this case of Korean American children's literature, basic questions such as the following must be addressed in the historical analysis:

- What are the authors' historical, social, and political backgrounds?
- How and why do the authors emphasize the sadness and difficulties of the Korean past? How do they contrast these to their "American" life?
- Why do you think such contrasts exist? Can you think of any examples that support or challenge such contrasts in your other readings about Korea, America, and Korean American society?

Such an analytical approach will create an inclusive space for children to practice communicating about Others' histories and cultures rather than essentially assuming that the heritage writer presents an authentic past or that there are embedded cultural differences between "American" and "immigrant American" communities.

REFERENCES

Constantakis, S. (2009). *Novels for students, volume 29: Presenting analysis, context, and criticism on commonly studied novels.* Detroit, MI: Gale.

Cumings, B. (1981). *The origins of the Korean War*. Princeton, NJ: Princeton University Press.
———. (1997). *Korea's place in the sun: A modern history*. New York: W. W. Norton.
Davis, R. (2004). Reinscribing (Asian) American history in Laurence Yep's *Dragonwings*. *The Lion and the Unicorn, 28*(3), 390–407.
Day, F. A. (1994). *Multicultural voices in contemporary literature: A resource for teachers*. Portsmouth, NH: Heinemann.
Kim, E. H. (1997). Korean American literature. In K. Cheung (Ed.), *An interethnic companion to Asian American literature* (156–91). Cambridge: Cambridge University Press.
Mastro, S. (1999). Teaching *Lost Names* in an American high school. *Education about Asia, 4*(2), 29–30.
Minear, R. H. (1999). *Lost Names*, master narratives, and messy history. *Education about Asia, 4*(2), 30–31.
Nelson, E. S. (2000). *Asian American novelists: A bio-bibliographical critical sourcebook*. Westport, CT: Greenwood Press.
Oh, A. H. (2015). *To save the children of Korea: The Cold War origins of international adoption*. Stanford, CA: Stanford University Press.
Park, M. L. (2007). Cold War legacies in Korean American children's literature. In L. Ousley (Ed.), *To see the wizard: Politics and the literature of childhood* (219–36). Newcastle upon Tyne, England: Cambridge Scholars.
Robinson, M. E. (2007). *Korea's twentieth-century odyssey*. Honolulu: University of Hawaii Press.
Scanlon, M. (2000). *Sook Nyul Choi (1937–)*. Westport, CT: Greenwood.
Sung, Y. K. (2009). "A post-colonial critique of the (mis)representation of Korean-Americans in children's picture books." (Unpublished doctoral dissertation). The University of Arizona.
Wee, S.-J., Park, S., & Choi, J. S. (2015). Korean culture as portrayed in young children's picture books: The pursuit of cultural authenticity. *Children's Literature in Education, 46*(1), 70–87.
Wright, P. R. (1999). Utilizing Richard Kim's *Lost Names* in the junior high classroom. *Education about Asia, 4*(2), 28–29.
Yi, J. (2014). "My heart beats in two places": Immigration stories in Korean-American picture books. *An International Quarterly, 45*(2), 129–44.
Yu, H. (2001). *Thinking Orientals: Migration, contact, and exoticism in modern America*. Oxford: Oxford University Press.
Yuh, J. (2005). Moved by war: Migration, diaspora, and the Korean War. *Journal of Asian American Studies, 8*(3), 277–91.

CHILDREN'S LITERATURE CITED

Choi, S. N. (1993). *Halmoni and the picnic*. Boston: Houghton Mifflin.
———. (1994). *Gathering of pearls*. Boston: Houghton Mifflin.

Choi, S. N., & Choi, S. N. (1991). *Year of impossible goodbyes*. Boston: Houghton Mifflin.

———. (1993). *Echoes of the white giraffe*. Boston: Houghton Mifflin.

Kim, D. (2008). *Long long time ago: Korean folk tales* (Rev. ed.). Elizabeth, NJ: Hollym International Corporation.

Kim, R. E. (1970). *Lost names: Scenes from a Korean boyhood*. New York: Praeger.

Kim, S. (2004). *Korean children's favorite stories*. Boston: Tuttle Pub.

Park, G., Jenkins, D. R., & Park, F. (1998). *My freedom trip*. Honesdale, PA: Boyds Mill Press.

Rattigan, K. (1998). *Dumpling soup*. Boston: Little, Brown.

Chapter 6

Reading with Cultural Empathy
Why Is It Difficult?
Yukari Takimoto Amos

In order to adapt and evolve with the growing diversity in classrooms, teachers must understand, be aware, and accept students from different ethnic and racial backgrounds. Developing empathy toward students who are culturally different from their own has been suggested as a promising way to promote the mutual understanding between various ethnic groups on both cognitive and affective levels (Wang et al., 2003). In the field of teaching, empathy is a professional disposition of effective teachers (Gordon, 1999). Thus, preparing teachers who are empathic with culturally different students is an important aspect of teacher preparation (Tettegah & Anderson, 2007).

In hopes of developing empathy toward cultural others who hold different viewpoints, customs, traditions, and more, teacher educators frequently require teacher candidates to read and discuss multicultural and international literature. Using cultural empathy as an analytical tool, this chapter presents a study that investigated white teacher candidates' interpretations of international children's stories from Japan. It delineates how problematic it was for teacher candidates to be empathic with Japanese cultural others and analyzes why it was difficult.

CULTURAL EMPATHY

Merriam-Webster's Collegiate Dictionary (n.d.) defines *empathy* as "the action of understanding, being aware of, being sensitive to, and vicariously experiencing the feelings, thoughts, and experience of another of either the past or present without having the feelings, thoughts, and experience fully communicated in an objectively explicit manner." According to this definition, *empathy* is understood as involving both intellectual and emotional domains. In light of cultural differences, however, it is crucial to expand the definition to include culture, thus to define cultural empathy.

Cultural empathy has two components. Intellectual empathy is the ability to "understand a racially or ethnically different person's thinking and/or feeling" (Wang et al., 2003, p. 222) and has two modalities. The first modality is imagining how cultural others are experiencing their conditions—in other words, the "imagine other" modality of perspective taking. The second modality is imagining how one would personally experience cultural others' conditions—in other words, the "imagine self" modality.

According to Warren (2014), two separate questions differentiate the two modalities: "What is the target feeling in this moment? (imagine other) versus how would I feel if I were the target in this moment? (imagine self)" (p. 397). The "imagine other" perspective most likely produces nonegoistic empathic responses because it requires that "the observer possess the capacity to surrender his or her own personal opinion, philosophies, beliefs, and points of view to embrace those of the target" (Warren, 2014, p. 397). Suppressing one's own egocentric perspectives and entertaining those of cultural others is an advanced cognitive process.

Another component of intellectual empathy—empathic emotions—refer to "the feeling of a person or persons from another ethnocultural group to the degree that one is able to feel the other's emotional condition from the point of view of that person's racial or ethnic culture" (Wang et al., 2003, p. 222). It is a person's emotional response to the emotional displays of cultural others. Empathic emotions, however, are considered incomplete if not accompanied with intellectual empathy. In other words, without highly sophisticated cognitive processes, mere sympathetic responses to others' emotional conditions does not constitute cultural empathy.

Our social and cultural perspectives based on our subjective identities—such as race, ethnicity, gender, socioeconomic status, and more—filter others' behaviors and attitudes. Therefore, we tend to judge cultural others based on what is right, appropriate, and good to us without taking into consideration that cultural others may have completely different sets of what is right, appropriate, and good, and that these differences are actually equal in status. Teachers' lack of experiences with diverse perspectives and unwillingness to submit themselves to the process of learning diverse perspectives may result in misunderstanding and misinterpreting students who are culturally different.

Teachers who have developed cultural empathy, however, can incorporate cultural others' diverse perspectives rather than dismissing them, and minimize adverse outcomes associated with misinterpretations of students' behaviors, engagement, and motivation (Warren, 2014). Teachers with this ability demonstrate culturally responsive teaching because they fully understand culturally accurate and socially appropriate perspectives of students, their families, and communities.

SETTING AND METHOD OF THE STUDY

Participants

Twenty-eight white teacher candidates (6 males and 22 females) who were enrolled in the teacher education program of a university in a rural area of the Pacific Northwest participated in the study. The majority of the participants majored in elementary education, while several others majored in PE, music, math, history, and chemistry.

All the participants read two children's literature stories from Japan (*Faithful Elephants*[1] and *Gongitsune*,[2] both translated in English) and answered the following questions for each story in an essay as a class assignment: (1) Make a short summery of the story; (2) What kind of themes or purposes do you think the story represents?; (3) Write your feelings freely after reading the story; (4) Would you read the story with the children in your future classroom?

Before reading the two stories, the participants were informed that both stories were famous and widely read among children in Japan at school and at home. For the synopsis of the stories, please see the notes at the end of the chapter.

Data Analysis

The essays the participants wrote were qualitatively analyzed with a particular focus on the following three questions: (1) the cognitive domain: Did the participants accurately interpret the theme and purpose of the story?; (2) the cognitive domain: Did the participants accurately interpret the main characters' feeling and behaviors from the cultural perspectives of the storytellers?; (3) the affective domain: What kinds of affect did the participants demonstrate about the characters and the stories? This process involved coding and then segregating the data by codes into data clumps for further analysis and description (Glesne, 2015).

In the end, all the codes were arranged into a logical order where several codes were clumped together in one thematic category.

WHITE TEACHER CANDIDATES' INTERPRETATIONS

The teacher candidates' responses show that they had difficulties developing empathy toward the protagonists in the two Japanese stories. The difficulties they experienced seem to be the direct cause of their misinterpretations of the stories.

Acknowledging But Resistant to Accepting Cultural Differences

Most children in Japan are familiar with the stories of *Faithful Elephants* and *Gongitsune*. Both are rather sad stories that involve the death of animals: in *Faithful Elephants*, three elephants in a zoo are starved to death by zookeepers, while in *Gongitsune*, one of the protagonists, Gon, the little fox, is accidentally shot to death by a farmer, Hyoju—another protagonist. The fact that both stories deal with death and do not end happily apparently gave a strong shock to the teacher candidates who were accustomed to reading stories with happy endings.

In addition, *Gongitsune*'s ambiguous story development style, which is different from that of US stories for children, confused and frustrated the teacher candidates. These cultural differences seem to have attributed to the teacher candidates' misinterpretations of the two stories.

Focus on Death

The teacher candidates' culture shock by reading the two sad Japanese stories could be summarized with such comments as, "I was surprised that this sort of material would present itself in a children's book," "Most of the stories in American culture generally have happy endings, or at least a happy turn at some point; however, this story started out depressing and just kept going," and "It's too frightening and dark."

Shocked with the fact that the two stories dealt with death up front, all the teacher candidates stated that they would not introduce the stories to the children in their future classrooms. One female student wrote, for example, "There would be little purpose sharing such a tragic story with the young population."

The teacher candidates' shock and their concomitant decision not to read the two stories in their future classroom seem to indicate that they took the "imagine self" perspective taking cognitive process. The fact that they asked themselves the question, "How would I feel if I were the protagonist in that situation?" was evident because the teacher candidates vigorously expressed their feelings of dislike and abhorrence toward the situations in the stories.

Their feelings were expressed with such comments as "The picture is a very graphic picture of the fox laying there dead in a puddle of blood, which is depressing," "I would have been very upset about the elephants dying," "If I had read this book as a child I would have cried because the ending was so sad," "The story about Gon really did upset me," and "This book about the elephants in Japan made me even more upset. I think it is because there was no happy ending and the entire story was about the death of the elephants."

Adjectives like *upsetting* and *depressing* that the teacher candidates used to describe their feelings after reading the stories indicate that they imagined themselves in the stories but did not like what they experienced, and that was why they felt that the stories were upsetting and depressing.

Because they themselves felt uncomfortable and unsettled about the stories, the teacher candidates' "imagine self" perspective went beyond the stories themselves and transcended to how children in their future classroom would feel and react after reading the two stories. For example, a male student wrote, "It may be horrifying to young children and would frighten them." Similar concerns were expressed, with comments below:

- "Children will probably be depressed for the rest of the day."
- "There was also a lot of death in the story that to some children might be extremely alarming or uncomfortable."
- "I feel that this book (*Faithful Elephants*) may be too upsetting for children."
- "I was saddened by the story and felt depressed after reading it, which is a way that I would not like to make a child feel."

The teacher candidates' sincere concern about young children's emotional state of being reflects how they viewed what children were capable of and what kind of storylines children's literature should contain. The view that children are innocent, fragile, and thus need to be sheltered from evil and harm that may provoke the feelings of sadness and scariness was represented in the comment, "Children are just too young and still learning to read for fun and not to be scared."

This view justified another perspective that children should read only fun and exciting stories with happy endings. A comment, "We should build our children up with positive expectations," symbolizes this outlook. Furthermore, the view of children being immature defined them as cognitively developing as well, and their cognitive underdevelopment was used to justify a perspective that children's stories should avoid ambiguous content and be simple in story lines in which heroes always defeat evil.

Along this same line, the teacher candidates expressed their concerns about whether or not American children would be able to comprehend the stories: "The students would have to be old enough to get past the sadness of the story," "It may be harder for younger students to understand what is happening," and "The story did not have any clear-cut meaning, especially not one that children could easily pick up on."

In the United States, death is indeed an uncommon topic in books for young children. The dominant folk theory dictates a view that "young children should be shielded from death because they lack the necessary affective and cognitive resources to cope with death" (Gutiérrez et al., 2014, p. 60). As a result, middle-class parents from the dominant racial group tend to avoid reading stories that represent death, and only a small number of white parents endorse the theory that young children have the psychological resources to handle death (Gutiérrez et al., 2014).

Therefore, the teacher candidates', all whites in this study, strong negative reactions to the two stories seems to be a logical consequence of being inculturated as a member of the dominant social group in US society. On the other hand, children's literature in East Asian nations (Japan, China, and South Korea) has begun to openly address death as a main theme since the 2000s (Lee et al., 2014). Lee et al. (2014) further contend that the literature in East Asia relies more on naturalistic aspects of death and focus on causal explanations.

What is striking is the fact that the teacher candidates cognitively understood that there were cultural differences between the United States and Japan with regard to the use of death in children's literature, as was represented in a comment, "It made me wonder if other cultures don't shelter their children as much as we do in our country." However, none of the teacher candidates gave evidence that they had attempted to understand the cultural perspectives of the Japanese adults and children who read these stories. In other words, the "imagine other" perspective did not seem to exist in the minds of these white US teacher candidates.

The absence of the "imagine other" perspective taken among the teacher candidates was evident when they attempted to mold the two stories to fit in their own cultural framework. First, they expressed a fierce desire to change the ending of each story so that the two stories would end happily—something they were familiar with. For example, a male student wrote, "They could have ended the story in a good way by Hyoju forgiving the fox for taking the eel." Another stated, "I feel it could have ended in a less horrifying way."

Second, some of them further felt it necessary to change the entire story line so that there would be no space for death to be present in the stories. For example, a female student wrote, "Why would a children's author write about death? How can the main character die?" Another female student wrote, "I am one of those people who like to read to escape reality and look for happy endings. There should never be stories with tragedy and the main character certainly should never die."

In this line of thinking, two compelling emotions coexist: a strong desire that stories be aligned with their familiar cultural framework for the sake of their own comfort, and an unwillingness to accept the Japanese cultural others' unfamiliar and disturbing story lines.

The absence of the "imagine other" perspective taking was also reflected in the teacher candidates' insistence on the US stories' superiority. Had the "imagine other" perspective been present, the insistence on their own cultures' superiority would most likely not have taken place because a vicarious experience with the Japanese cultural others would have certainly enticed empathy, thus reducing these egocentric viewpoints.

The demonstration of superiority ranged from negative, such as "A typical American children's literature story does not have nearly this much death," to ethnocentric, "I had a hard time accepting this as a piece of children's literature. There was no happy ending, no exciting parts to the story; it was just facts about a horrific event."

Some comments were openly jingoistic: "In American books, if the main character/hero does experience a hardship, like death of a parent, the character prevails by the end of the story. I do not see how this would not be a better option for younger children," and "It makes me feel like American children's literature wants to not crush a child's happy feelings, whereas Japanese children's literature tends toward desensitizing their youth."

Other comments were completely dismissive: "I can find other international children's literature stories that are not so depressing for children in this age group."

The superiority of US children's stories in the minds of the teacher candidates was effectively demonstrated when several teacher candidates used prescriptive language to invalidate the merit of the two Japanese children's stories. Since it was obvious which countries were in comparison, the act of invalidating the Japanese stories naturally elevated the US stories' superior positioning.

First, the teacher candidates reiterated that children should be shielded from sad stories and not experience emotional disturbances such as sadness. A female student noted, "I don't think that young children, who are so innocent and imaginative, should be exposed to the dark realities of the world at such a young age." In this comment, the student criticized the two Japanese stories for not only revealing "the dark realities of the world"—death and war—but also damaging the purity and innocence of young children. As a result, this student manifested her belief that the US stories were in comparison superior.

Similarly, a male student noted: "As educators, are we not trying to keep innocence within the grasp of children for as long as we possibly can? This book (*Gongitsune*) steers away from innocent thinking by the deaths of not only one, but two animals. Children can learn lessons in a book without a death of animals or a main character." In effect, this comment not only critiqued the exposure of young children to death but also suggested an absence of morale in Japanese teachers for presenting material of this sort.

Both students' comments highlight the presence of American whiteness—it functions as the unnamed, universal moral referent by which all others are evaluated, measured, and defined (Chubbuck, 2004; Frankenberg, 1993).

Clearly, the teacher candidates determined that the two Japanese stories lacked positive educational value because points of the story were made in a grim manner.

For example, a male student wrote, "I understand the purpose of the story is to enforce the negative points of war, but I felt that the author went through unnecessary lengths to make the content more disturbing than needed." Another stated that the stories unnecessarily helped to habituate children to violence: "I find it unfortunate because children, although should be aware of some things, shouldn't be corrupted with guns and death. It sets up children to accept this way of thinking, which I find wrong," and "The details about Gon's mother dying, Hyoju getting beaten up, Hyoju's mother dying, and then Gon getting killed are all emotionally trying. These are difficult issues to talk about. This story isn't the best way to introduce these topics."

Another student's criticism seems to summarize the feelings of this group of white American teacher candidates, "I do not understand why children should read this book. Children can learn about grief from things other than reading about starving elephants. I feel like this is too harsh for children." In all their comments the teacher candidates indirectly but clearly stated that US children's stories were superior because they lacked the death and violence depicted in these Japanese children's stories.

Culturally Unfamiliar Story Development Style

US children's stories tend to progress in a linear way: an introduction, main parts, and a clear ending, with causes and effects clearly marked. In a study on the effects of culture on writing practices, Kaplan (1972) symbolized the American pattern as a straight arrow pointing down the page, while the "Oriental" pattern was symbolized as an inward turning spiral. Several East Asian scholars describe the American style as explicit and direct, while the East Asian style as implicit and indirect (Lu, 1998; Gao & Ting-Toomey, 1998). The same scholars further explain that words alone are inadequate to capture all aspects of thoughts, feelings, or experiences.

On the other hand, American students are often told that if they can't put something into words, they don't really understand it (de Vries, 2002). Between the United States and Japan, there seems to be differences in how much words are used to convey meaning and how much other factors are involved to accomplish the same purpose. This cultural difference allows Japanese children to tolerate a higher degree of ambiguity and implicitness in stories compared to their US counterparts.

The dominance of words in interpreting was evident when a female student wrote, "Because of the author's last reference to the gun, I was more drawn to the gun than Gon." In this comment, it appears that the student's attention went straight to the gun because she read the word *gun* in the text. This particular cultural preference—a reliance on words—provided the teacher candidates with a significantly difficult reading, resulting in extremely unexpected interpretations in *Gongitsune*.

The ending of the story seems to have attributed to this cause. The ending of *Gongitsune* is a profoundly powerful one from the Japanese cultural perspective. In *Gongitsune*, the death of Gon, the little fox, is announced not through the word *death* but with a combination of the two phrases *gun smoke* and *Gon lying down on the floor*. By intentionally avoiding the word *death* and relying only on the depiction of the scene, the impact of Gon's death intensifies, thus shock and sadness also climax, leaving the reader with more nuanced, nebulous, and complex emotions.

The Japanese reader, at this moment, most likely feels sympathetic to Gon, who attempted to amend his past wrongdoings only to be shot to death by Hyoju, whom he felt obligated to help after the death of Hyoju's mother, which Gon felt partially responsible for. At the same time, the same degree of sympathy goes to Hyoju who mistakenly shot Gon without realizing that it was Gon who was bringing food to him all along.

The sympathetic feelings toward both protagonists who kept miscommunicating and never understood each other's intentions naturally entice an empathic feeling in which the reader shares pains with the protagonists. The reader's wistful realization that nothing could restore the situation further deepens the empathy toward the protagonists.

The same ending, however, was too implicit, ambiguous, and nebulous from the teacher candidates' cultural perspective. For example, a male student wrote, "There is not enough of a conclusion to this book to state why it is a valid children's tale." Another male student stated, "I am not sure what purpose it serves whether or not it is just a cultural and societal attribute." These comments underline the teacher candidates' frustration toward a story that does not display clear-cut meanings and conclude with a simple, positive ending.

The following comment by a female student represents the feelings of this group of US students who were frustrated by the story's moral complexity:

> *Gongitsune* was confusing and difficult to follow. It brings the reader through a roller-coaster of emotions as Gon goes from happy to sad to mischievous. It was muddy under several different elements and twists. The relationship with Hyoju was confusing and inconsistent. Hyoju was an ally for Gon at the beginning, but in the end, killed Gon. The terms of conditions were coincidental, especially since Gon was actually saving Hyoju's life, all while Hyoju took Gon's life. The multiple morals and twists make it difficult to follow, and seem to counteract each other with the complexity.

The comment above suggests this student's desire for a simple story line where good and evil are clearly demarcated, where good remains good from the beginning to the end, and where the story does not contain unexpected twists and turns.

The teacher candidates' frustration toward *Gongitsune*'s ambiguity indicates that they acknowledged the cultural difference in a story development style between the United States and Japan but were resistant to accepting the Japanese style as legitimate.

It appears that among the teacher candidates who encountered the significant cultural difference in a story development style, a desire to make themselves comfortable with their own familiar cultural style was stronger than the act of attempting to understand an unfamiliar cultural style. If they had taken the "imagine other" perspective, the teacher candidates would have considered why the two stories are widely read in Japan despite the obvious differences in styles of children's literature that they were familiar with.

They could have further pondered why the Japanese people would tolerate moral ambiguity in children's stories, and finally might have concluded that the Japanese cultural others would have felt the same way about their direct and explicit story development style used in US children's stories. However, little evidence of curiosity about Japanese culture was found in the observations of the teacher candidates when commenting about these stories.

Paying Critical Attention to Actions, Not Emotions

The lack of the "imagine other" perspective taking was further evidenced by the teacher candidates' lack of attention to the protagonists' feelings. Had the "imagine other" perspective been present, the teacher candidates would have surely pondered what the protagonists were feeling at certain points of time and consequently may have displayed sympathetic and empathic feelings toward them, particularly since all the protagonists in the two Japanese stories struggled emotionally.

In reality, the primary focus of the two stories is not death. Instead, the stories portray the dilemmas, agonies, miscommunications, and misunderstandings of the protagonists in each story. The teacher candidates' absence of attention to the protagonists' feelings was striking, while most made one-dimensional critiques of the protagonists' actions.

Faithful Elephants

In *Faithful Elephants*, the zookeepers' action of letting the elephants starve to death was met with harsh comments from the teacher candidates: "Starvation is probably one of the most horrendous ways to die because it is so prolonged," and "It seemed inhumane to make those elephants suffer that way and the elephants did not understand why they were being tortured."

In these comments, the teacher candidates focused on the elephants' death through starvation but completely ignored the pain the zookeepers felt when they ran out of food for the animals during the war, could find no humane way to kill them, and needed to endure the pain of witnessing their beloved elephants experience a slow, wasting death.

The teacher candidates were unable to comprehend the situation the zookeepers were in and were adamant that there must have been alternates during the war other than letting the elephants die. Their options included "moving the elephants to a more secure area," "selling the elephants to a zoo in another country," "transporting the elephants in a cargo plane," "shipping them to another country by plane or by boat," "using a tranquilizer gun," and "shooting them." Their optimistic suggestions for the alternatives highlight the teacher candidates' ignorance of the conditions faced by Tokyo during the war.

In reality, it was impossible to move the elephants from heavily bombed Tokyo even to a nearby city. It would probably have caused more chaos to the city by doing so. It was also impossible to use a rifle to kill the elephants because the Japanese Imperial Army confiscated all the weapons.

The following comments illustrate the teacher candidates' lack of knowledge about life in Tokyo during World War II, which was heavily bombed:

- "I wondered why they didn't just risk having part of the zoo getting hit and letting the animals out? If the city was already being bombed, it's hard to think how much worse it would be if some elephants got out into the city."
- "The lack of creativity on the part of the zookeepers. To me, it seemed like they had already given up before they really exhausted all other options. I don't understand why they needed to kill the elephants at all. If the elephants were to escape the zoo, they may cause a little damage but in reality the entire city was being bombed in the first place."

When their comments focused on the zookeepers, the teacher candidates described them as weak and morally corrupt human beings. The teacher candidates described the zookeepers as "acting foolishly and downright stupid," "acted on it too quickly," "it was a brash decision on the part of the zoo keepers. I thought the zoo keepers were pretty heartless to ignore the obvious suffering of the elephants," "betraying the elephants they liked like their own family," and "I wondered what the elephants might have been thinking as they lay there dying wondering why the zoo keepers were ignoring them."

Some of them expanded the zookeepers to the entire Japanese population and made such a comment as "From an American perspective, thoughts about Japanese folks are usually harsh and insensitive because of the war."

None of the teacher candidates showed an interest in the zookeepers' inner feelings, their agony at witnessing their beloved elephants slowly dying, their remorse for making a painful decision, their helpless condition in which they had no resources to alleviate the elephants' pain, their dilemma of saving people at the sacrifice of animals, and their anger toward the seemingly endless war. None of this registered in the teacher candidates' minds.

Without attempting to experience the zookeepers' complex inner feelings, the teacher candidates were neither able to sympathize nor to empathize with the zookeepers. They depicted the zookeepers as one-dimensional, evil, insensitive people. Their depiction of the zookeepers ultimately elevated the teacher candidates' own moral positioning.

In this sense, it is logical that the teacher candidates evaluated *Faithful Elephants* as a story of animal cruelty and abuse with such comments, "I find it hard to believe that anyone could do something so cruel. I guess being raised in America I see it as animal abuse and to me there is never a good reason to abuse an animal in such a way," and "I know that the zookeepers did not want to abuse the elephants, but that is exactly what it was. Animal abuse just makes me sick. I can't stand it. It's terrible that the human species, who have the ability to reason, could make a choice to starve an animal that is so helpless."

A Japanese story that conveys multiple and sometimes contradictory complex emotions of human beings to let children know the grief, fear, and sadness caused by the war was simply interpreted as a mere story of animal abuse by the teacher candidates who refused to introspect the moral dilemmas and struggles of the zookeepers.

Gongitsune

The teacher candidates' tendency to pay attention to the actions made by the protagonists but not their emotions was also apparent in the ways they interpreted *Gongitsune*'s main theme. The teacher candidates concluded that *Gongitsune* portrayed the consequence of stealing and the importance of anger management. This conclusion seems to be the result of attempting to desperately find something concrete to teach young children out of the ambiguity of the story. This is because children's literature is closely related to a pedagogy that views stories as a powerful means for educating children (Nikolajeva, 2016).

In the story, Gon is known as a mischievous fox who steals food from the villagers. Since stealing is not considered morally good, Gon's repeated act of stealing was taken as a point of moral teaching to young children by the teacher candidates. They made such comments as, "Stealing is wrong, even if it is intended to be helpful," and "Teach little kids the value of not stealing."

This moral point of teaching was further directly associated with Gon's death to teach young children the consequence of stealing. For example, a female student wrote, "Since Gon was obviously not good, it was inevitable for him to dig himself in an irreversible hole." Another female student stated, "If you steal you die. It seems an extremely harsh moral but at least it follows a normal story pattern."

In the comments above, it is evident that the teacher candidates focused on Gon's actions rather than his emotions and consequently condemned Gon for stealing rather than deeply engaging themselves in Gon's inner struggles of not being understood by Hyoju. Rather, the teacher candidates detected a clear cause and effect in Gon's actions and determined that Gon deserved to die because of his immoral actions. This Calvinistic thinking seems to have given the teacher candidates a comfort because it was a "normal" consequence for them and a "normal" story development pattern they were familiar with.

What was lacking, however, was even the slightest imagination of what Gon was going through and how he was feeling. Preoccupied with trying to understand the story in their "normal" way, the teacher candidates neglected to see how intertwined and inseparable Gon's actions and emotions were. A focus only on Gon's actions, thus, resulted in superficial and inaccurate interpretations.

Anger management was another theme the teacher candidates came up with. The teacher candidates condemned Hyoju for mistakenly and hastily killing Gon and acting on his anger and impulse.

This theme was apparent in the comments like, "I thought there was a better way Hyoju could have handled his anger at Gon in the end, instead of just shooting him," "I wanted to yell out to Hyoju, 'No, you don't know what you are doing. You are judging Gon out of your anger instead of understanding his heart.' Hyoju killing Gon seemed so unjust," "Control your temper and do not act while having the temper. Consequences of acting out of anger," and "It confused me about how Hyoju acted on impulse when he killed Gon. I am guessing this incident equaled to a moral of not acting on impulse and making sure to get all information gathered before making decisions." These comments clearly illustrate the teacher candidates' interpretation of the theme "think before acting" after reading *Gongitsune*.

Several teacher candidates further included hunting as the theme of *Gongitsune*. A male student, for example, stated, "Hunting seems to be a theme in Gon. This story brings to light the side of hunting that most hunters don't consider." A female student wrote, "We need to be more conscientious when hunting to ensure that we are not killing a mother with a baby."

In the teacher candidates' mind, Hyoju's action of killing Gon was unbelievable. The slightest possibility that they could be acting upon their imminent impulse was nonexistent among the teacher candidates, which seems to have been the result of their taking the "imagine self" perspective only. The absolute absence of this possibility suggests that the teacher candidates had a firm belief of their own moral superiority over the protagonists in *Gongitsune*. They were convinced that they would absolutely never act like Hyoju.

Because of their strong desire to read the story in their familiar way and an equally strong belief that they would remain morally good under any circumstances, the teacher candidates seem to have psychologically distanced themselves from Gon and Hyoju, who showed immorality and displayed weak personalities. This psychological distance naturally allowed the teacher candidates not to take the "imagine other" perspective.

Without considering the protagonists' dilemmas and agonies that could have been obtained via the "imagine other" perspective taking, the teacher candidates felt neither sympathy nor empathy, and the absence of the empathic feeling seems to have been the result of their strictly action-oriented interpretations.

DISCUSSIONS

In order to truly understand and interpret international children's literature from Japan, the teacher candidates needed to take the "imagine other" perspective taking cognitive process in which they intellectually analyze the significant and subtle cultural traits that contrast markedly with their own and feel how another culture feels from the standpoint of the insider (Hanvey, 2001). Therefore, the teacher candidates' series of misinterpretations of *Faithful Elephants* and *Gongitsune* is an indication that they did not develop cultural empathy at the cognitive level. We need to ask what caused this failure.

The primary cause seems to be condensed with the teacher candidates' positive and superior orientation toward the self. Although acknowledging that there were significant cultural differences between the United States and Japan, the teacher candidates were adamant about what was "right" and what should have taken place from their own cultural framework. This firm stance consequently made them denounce, denigrate, invalidate, and reject the Japanese cultural others.

For example, the teacher candidates openly rejected the stories that involved death and contended that children's stories should never deal with death and should always end happily. This seems to be a logical consequence of holding an intrinsic belief in their own positivity and superiority, which naturally defines any differences as negative, inferior, and abnormal. Because the Japanese cultural others were perceived and defined as inferior and abnormal, it appears that there was no necessity for the teacher candidates to consider Japanese cultural perspectives.

In addition, the teacher candidates' rejection of the Japanese story development style seems to not only directly reflect on their positive and superior orientation toward the self but also manifest their entitlement to surrounding themselves. The Japanese story development style of conveying messages without necessarily using words is sharply different from that of the American style of conveying messages strictly with words.

It was obvious that the teacher candidates were baffled with this particular cultural difference, were confused with how the story progressed, particularly in *Gongitsune*, and consequently were frustrated. Their blunt rejection of the Japanese story development style as illegitimate suggests that they prioritized their own comfort and convenience over their effort to comprehend the cultural others' perspectives.

The superior orientation toward the self was most strikingly displayed by the teacher candidates' keen and critical attention to the protagonists' actions but their complete absence of the protagonists' feelings. Because the teacher candidates firmly believed in their own moral superiority, they naturally paid attention to the protagonists' moral inferiority, which was displayed by their actions.

At the same time, they ignored the protagonists' complex feelings. Since it is indeed impossible to comprehend the complex stories of *Faithful Elephants* and *Gongitsune* without feeling emphatic toward the protagonists, it is no wonder that the absence of the "imagine other" perspective taking by the teacher candidates resulted in the ways they evaluated the two stories with such simple terms as animal abuse, the consequence of stealing, and anger management.

Two other factors appear to have further contributed to the teacher candidates' misinterpretations. Their ignorance of the history of Japan seems to have prohibited them from feeling emphatic with the protagonists in the two Japanese stories. In other words, if they had possessed more accurate knowledge about the conditions of Japan and Japanese people during World War II, the teacher candidates could have interpreted the stories in more authentic ways. In this sense, knowledge seems to play a role in reducing prejudice (Allport, 1979), and enhancing knowledge about cultural others seems to be a precursor for developing cultural empathy (Pettigrew & Tropp, 2008).

Another factor is a perceived social distance between the United States and Asia. Western and Asian countries are said to hold maximum sociocultural differences (Samovar et al., 2014). Breuning (2007) further contends that international students from Asia and Africa face a higher likelihood of being perceived as vastly culturally different than students from other regions in the world by white Americans due to significant discrepancies in language, culture, and communication styles. This perception could have influenced the teacher candidates' interpretations negatively.

Overall, it appears that both ethnocentrism (valuing of one's ethnic/cultural group over others) and monoculturalism (belief in one "right" culture) were strongly present in the ways the white teacher candidates interpreted the two Japanese stories.

CONCLUSION

This chapter analyzes how the white teacher candidates interpreted *Faithful Elephants* and *Gongitsune*—children's stories from Japan—with a focus on whether or not they developed cultural empathy toward the stories and the protagonists.

The findings of the study indicate that the teacher candidates had tremendous difficulty authentically interpreting the stories. Their misinterpretations seem to have been guided by their strong sense of superiority toward the self. The chapter warns that although introducing international children's literature from Asia is commendable, it could end up in invalidating the literature if not accompanied by culturally authentic interpretations.

NOTES

1. Synopsis of *Faithful Elephants: A True Story of Animals, People, and War*, by Y. Tsuchiya. Illustrated by T. Lewin. Boston: Houghton Mifflin, 1997.

During the bleak and miserable last days of World War II, Tokyo was showered with bombs. "If the zoo were destroyed, the animals might be freed accidentally and wreak havoc on the city." This was the imminent fear the authorities had at that time. They eventually decided that all the zoo animals should be killed to avoid this disaster. One by one, the animals lives ended at the zoo except for the elephants. The elephants would refuse to eat the poisonous food the zookeepers offered. Their thick skin would not allow the needles in the syringes that contained poison to penetrate either.

The only option left to the zookeepers who had attended the elephants with much care was to have them starve to death.

2. Synopsis of *Gongitsune (Gon, the Little Fox)*, by N. Nimmi. Illustrated by M. Genjirou. New York: Museyon, 1932.

Gon, a little and lonely fox, repeatedly steals food at a little village and creates other mischief, constantly making the villagers angry. One day Gon steals an eel from Hyoju, which Hyoju wanted to give to his dying mother. His mother subsequently dies without eating an eel before her death, and Hyoju blames Gon for not being able to feed his mother an eel she wished to eat.

Gon realizes that he made a mistake and tries to amend by secretly giving Hyoju food that he actually steals from other villagers. But the villagers accuse Hyoju of stealing their food and beat him up. Afterward, Gon only gives mushrooms and nuts he himself collects in the forest. Hyoju is grateful for the food but does not know who brings them.

One day, Hyoju sees Gon sneaking around his house and shoots him out of anger about his mother's death, only to discover it was Gon who kept bringing the food. *Gongitsune* is the winner of the 2016 USSB outstanding international book.

REFERENCES

Allport, G. W. (1979). *The nature of prejudice* (2nd ed.). Reading, MA: Addison-Wesley.
Breuning, M. (2007). Undergraduate international students: A resource for the intercultural education of American peers? *College Student Journal, 41*(4), 1114–22.
Chubbuck, S. M. (2004). Whiteness enacted, whiteness disrupted: The complexity of personal congruence. *American Educational Research Journal, 41*(2), 301–33.
De Vries, K. (2002). "Writing "clearly": Differing perceptions of clarity in Chinese and American texts." Proceedings of the International Symposium on Contrastive and Translation Studies between Chinese and English, Shanghai, PRC. Retrieved from https://stuff.mit.edu/people/kdevries/clarity2a.pdf.
Empathy. (n.d.). In *Merriam-Webster's online dictionary* (11th ed.). Retrieved from https://www.merriam-webster.com/dictionary/empathy.
Frankenberg, R. (1993). *The social construction of whiteness: White women, race matters*. Minneapolis: The University of Minnesota Press.
Gao, G., & Ting-Toomey, S. (1998). *Communicating effectively with the Chinese*. Thousand Oaks, CA: Sage Publications.
Glesne, C. (2015). *Becoming a qualitative researcher* (5th ed.). Boston: Pearson/Allyn and Bacon.
Gordon, G. L. (1999). Teacher talent and urban schools. *Phi Delta Kappan, 81*(4), 304–7.
Gutiérrez, I. T., Miller, P. J., Rosengren, S., & Schein, S. S. (2014). Affective dimensions of death: Children's books, questions, and understandings. *Monographs of the Society for Research in Child Development, 79*(1), 43–61.
Hanvey, R. G. (2001). An attainable global perspective. In P. E. O'Meara, H. D. Mehlinger, & R. M. Newman (Eds.), *Changing perspectives on international education* (pp. 219–25). Bloomington: Indiana University Press.
Kaplan, R. B. (1972). *The anatomy of rhetoric: Prolegomena to a functional theory of rhetoric: Essays for teachers*. Philadelphia, PA: Center for Curriculum Development.
Lee, J. S., Kim, E. Y., Choi, Y, & Koo, J. H. (2014). Cultural variances in composition of biological and supernatural concepts of death: A content analysis of children's literature. *Death Studies, 38*(8), 538–45.

Lu, X. (1998). *Rhetoric in ancient China: Fifth to third century B.C.E.: A Comparison with classical Greek rhetoric.* Columbia, SC: University of South Carolina Press.

Nikolajeva, M. (2016). *Children's literature comes of age: Toward a new aesthetic.* New York: Routledge.

Pettigrew, T. F., & Tropp, L. R. (2008). How does intergroup contact reduce prejudice?: Meta-analytic tests of three mediators. *European Journal of Social Psychology, 38*(6), 922–34.

Ridley, C. R., & Lingle, D. W. (1996). Cultural empathy in multicultural counseling: A multidimensional process model. In P. B. Pedersen & J. G. Draguns (Eds.) (4th ed.), *Counseling across cultures* (pp. 21–46). Thousand Oaks, CA: Sage.

Samovar, L., Porter, R. E., McDaniel, E. R., & Roy, C. S. (Eds.) (2014). *Intercultural communication: A reader* (14th ed.). Boston: Cengage Learning.

Tettegah, S., & Anderson, C. J. (2007). Pre-service teachers' empathy and cognitions: Statistical analysis of text data by graphical models. *Contemporary Educational Psychology, 32*(1), 48–82.

Wang, Y., Davidson, M. M., Yakushko, O. F., Savoy, H. B., Tan, J. A., & Bleier, J. K. (2003). The scale of ethnocultural empathy: Development, validation, and reliability. *Journal of Counseling Psychology, 50*(2), 221–34.

Warren, C. A. (2014). Towards a pedagogy for the application of empathy in culturally diverse classrooms. *Urban Review, 46*(3), 395–419.

Chapter 7

Reading Analytically and Feeling Connected

When Indonesian Preservice Teachers Read Foreign Stories from China, Iraq, and the United States

Tati Lathipatud Durriyah

Research on reader response in education often views preservice teachers as a context in which children's responses to literature may emerge; in other words, preservice teachers are viewed as persons who provide opportunities for literary response. Not much attention, however, has been given to understanding the kinds of literary responses that may emerge from preservice teachers. This chapter examines the literary responses of a group of Indonesian preservice teachers to children's literature from cultures that were foreign to them: China, Iraq, and the United States.

TEACHERS IN READER RESPONSE RESEARCH

A substantial body of research attempts to make better sense of readers' responses to literature. Research on readers' responses to literature (e.g., Marshall, 2000) describes the benefits of literature that encompass more than just the reader's aesthetic pleasure. Reading literature also supports students' nonliterary academic achievement, such as an increased understanding of nonreading-related subjects such as social studies. Further, multicultural literature influences the beliefs of students about social issues.

As for the reader, factors such as the reader's age and gender matter. Younger readers engage with the story action while older readers are more engaged with characters and their psychological aspects, while a reader's gender influences perceptual orientations when responding to text (Marshall,

2000). In short, a range of variation in readers' responses to literature has been examined.

Nevertheless, there is a conspicuous gap in reader response research. The majority of the research focuses on reader responses at the primary and secondary levels; only a handful of studies were conducted with teachers (Marshall, 2000; Roser, Martinez, & Wood, 2011).

What is more, literary response research generally identifies teachers as part of a context in which responses may occur (Marshall, 2000). Research only considers teachers' "moves" or chosen pedagogies or strategies and how they position students to respond in order to derive literary meaning making (Roser, Martinez, & Wood, 2011), while the perspective of teachers as readers is relatively neglected.

We have learned from available research on teachers' reader response that we cannot simply assume that preservice teachers who want to be literature teachers take pleasure from literary reading (Draper, Barksdale-Ladd, & Radencich, 2000). Teachers need to have opportunities to engage in book discussions and open up their own stories in reading (Wolf, Ballertine, & Hill, 2000).

Rosenblatt (2005) declares, "Every reading act is a transaction involving a particular reader, a text, and occurring in a particular context" (p. 7). Rosenblatt's remark proceeds from an assumption that humans internalize language through a transactional process with a particular environment. Reader response theory is credited for encouraging teachers and researchers to examine the nature of readers' experiences with literature and what their responses tell us about the experiences that they draw upon in meaning making.

Reader response theory suggests that the ways in which preservice teachers respond to literature indicate their goals as future teachers (Brenner, 2003; Wolf, 2001). Preservice teachers who study literature would gain knowledge of literature (Floden & Meniketti, 2005). Preservice teachers' experiences of responding to literature may likely influence how they might perceive the role of literature in their future teaching (Asselin, 2000). In short, studying literature helps future teachers shape their teaching practices.

STUDY

This chapter describes a study in which Indonesian preservice teachers' responses to international stories were investigated. The researcher sought to discover how Indonesian preservice teachers responded to foreign children's literature being read aloud and what aspects of social and culture influence their responses to foreign children's literature.

Research Design and Participants

The research design employed in the study was based on the tradition of teachers as researchers (Mills, 2007). The author conducted the study in a class she taught at a state Islamic university in Jakarta, Indonesia. Because many of the literary works used were written in English, participants were selected based on a passing level of English reading proficiency (similar to a 400 score on a paper-based TOEFL test) that was evaluated prior to university admission. Eleven preservice students participated in the study.

Data Sources and Analysis

Two primary data sources of the study were video recordings and the participants' reflective journals. The author selected picture books for the participants to read, invited them to respond to and discuss the stories, and videotaped the read-aloud activities. After each read-aloud session the participants wrote a reflection paper about the books and the related discussions.

The study attempted to investigate the Indonesian preservice teachers' responses to the picture books from cultures and countries different from their own. In order to do so, the author referred to Sipe's (2000, 2008) work on picture book response. Sipe developed a framework of literary response categories for picture books. Drawing from years of classroom research, Sipe (2000, 2008) proposes five conceptual categories that emerged from students' verbal responses during read-aloud sessions: analytical, intertextual, personal, transparent, and performative.

In particular, the present study focused on two categories: analytical and personal connections. An analytical reading occurs when a reader attempts to describe, evaluate, infer, and predict stories and illustrations, including the elements of structures and illustrations, story summary, and characters. For example, a reader focuses on the sequence of an illustration and evaluates the logic of the sequence.

A personal connection occurs when a reader calls attention to personal experiences and feelings and reflects on them in order to make sense of a story. A story that allows readers to connect personally has the potential to not only inform but also transform the lives of readers. This is exemplified in Sipe's (2008) description about a young reader who was referring to a storybook read-aloud and its subsequent discussion to envision his future life.

Data analysis involved reading through the participants' weekly journals and identifying comments deemed relevant to the research questions. I then reviewed the video recordings by focusing on incidents relevant to the participants' journal entries. I looked for common themes and created a narrative description using the participants' own words. In a later stage of data analysis, I explicated a range of themes included in these findings. For example, when the participants discussed the picture books, I looked for related sub-themes, such as illustrations and authors/illustrators.

Picture Books Selected in the Study

Artistic pleasure and benefit gained from picture books are not solely based on the literary aspect of their narrative. Picture books offer readers an aesthetic experience through both visual art and written narrative (Kiefer, 2008; Sipe, 2000). I took the visual as well as narrative aspects of international picture books as the main criteria for selecting three books to use in this study.

The selected picture books were from China (*Yeh-Shen: A Cinderella Story from China*), from Iraq (*The Librarian of Basra*), and from the United States (*Of Thee I Sing*).

Yeh-Shen is a Chinese version of the Cinderella story. It shares some familiar elements yet contains different story lines and ending as well. Ed Young illustrated an intriguing representation of ancient imperial China. Written and illustrated by Jeanette Winter, *The Librarian of Basra* tells a true story about an extraordinary heroine named Alia Muhammad Baker, the chief librarian in Basra, Iraq. Alia's great courage helped to rescue almost the entire library collection days before it was set on fire.

Of Thee I Sing is written by Barack Obama and is illustrated by Loren Long. The book is a collection of illustrated letters from Obama to his daughters and describes American national figures who have shaped the nation, such as the deaf-blind activist Helen Keller, Abraham Lincoln, and the Native American leader Sitting Bull.

PRESERVICE TEACHERS' RESPONSES TO STORIES FROM CHINA, IRAQ, AND THE UNITED STATES

The Indonesian preservice teachers all seemed to enjoy the stories from China, Iraq, and the United States by making both analytical and personal connections. At the same time, some misinterpretations and evidence of misreading were also detected.

Yeh-Shen: A Cinderella Story from China

After the passing of her father, Yeh-Shen is left to live with a stepmother and a stepsister. Motivated by jealousy over Yeh-Shen's fine features, the stepfamily badly mistreats her. They kill Yeh-Shen's beloved pet fish. She cries in mourning for her only companion. Yeh-Shen cries again when she loses one of her golden shoes as she had promised her fish guardian that she would not lose them.

The character of Yeh-Shen generated mixed opinions from the Indonesian preservice teachers. The majority (9 out of 11) judged Yeh-Shen as "very weak" for not defending herself against the stepmother and the sister's cruel treatment. One preservice teacher remarked, "I dislike that kind of [weak] personality. We must be strong in facing all problems. Don't cry easily because it will only encourage others to bother us even more."

Others, however, were more sympathetic toward Yeh-Shen and offered some justification for her seemingly weak attitude. For example, one preservice teacher stated:

When Yeh-Shen cried, it showed that she had a pure heart. There was nothing she could do except cry. I think she was not weak, but she tried to relieve her pain by crying. I also believe that crying is the easiest way to relieve my burden and pain.

The comments above occurred at a point during the course when the preservice teachers had just began to become familiar with the practice of giving a personal response to a story. Many of them initially struggled to write a story response based on an honest and personal reading, and they made a story summary instead. As the course progressed, they were more comfortable with offering personal connections, as exemplified in that particular quote from the preservice teacher whose response was thoughtful and empathetic.

Notably, when the class discussed *Yeh-Shen*, the preservice teachers' opinions about the main character, Yeh-Shen, differed. While many still came up with a shallow interpretation of Yeh-Shen, calling her weak, others had a deeper reading and offered more empathetic interpretations about her. These different responses indicate different levels of personal connections: to some participants, the connection to the story was strong, while to others, it was not.

Illustrations in the book also contributed to differences in levels of personal connections among the preservice teachers. Some participants were impressed with Ed Young's "artistic" and "meaningful" illustrations. One participant said, "The pictures are complicated; we couldn't predict the story from the pictures without reading the text." This comment suggests that the preservice teachers enjoyed looking at the pictures that were culturally unfamiliar and different from them, and found such pictures' complexity pleasing, ultimately triggering their analytical responses.

An example of analytical response was demonstrated by the preservice teachers' curiosity toward Chinese culture. In particular, symbols in the book's illustrations appear to have sparked the most curiosity. One notable symbol was a fish. In the book, still mourning for her dead fish, Yeh-Shen gathers its remaining bones. Yeh-Shen then hears a voice of an old man telling her to keep the bones and kneel to the bones whenever Yeh-Shen needs something. The illustration of the old man resembles the shape of a giant fish.

One preservice teacher said, "In *Yeh-Shen*, the illustrator put something that became a symbol of China (the koi fish). The fish became a fairy godmother. I think people in China regarded the koi fish as a source of luck." As this comment indicates, this particular preservice teacher seems to have analyzed the important role a fairy godmother plays in the story in association with a significant meaning the koi fish holds in the Chinese culture. With the help of the illustration, she obtained new cultural information different from her own.

Slippers or shoes comprised another cultural symbol that conveyed a cross-cultural meaning. The book describes the slippers to be tiny and perfectly formed to Yeh-Shen's tiny feet. Discussions about Yeh-Shen's sparkling slippers led to another discussion about the past tradition of binding women's feet in China—women with small feet were more desirable in China.

This discussion seemed to connect with a preservice teacher called Yanti's experience of buying shoes in a Chinese-owned store in Indonesia. Yanti recalled:

> I also have small feet, and I used to feel ashamed of them. Then one day I went to a shoe store owned by a Chinese man. He said that I was so lucky to have small feet. Women in China had to bind their feet in order to make them smaller. Men in China regarded women with small feet as more beautiful. Since then, I've never felt ashamed again with my small feet.

Due to her own experience, the cultural significance of small feet in China made more sense to Yanti. For this particular participant, *Yeh-Shen*'s illustrations sparked her interest, which seemed to have contributed to her reading the story more analytically and empathetically as well.

To some extent, this finding appears to confirm Cotton's (2000) argument that for foreign readers, an illustrated book provides a venue of learning that transcends cultural and linguistic barriers. Cotton (2000) insists that for children from diverse backgrounds, picture book illustrations could potentially facilitate learning the "love of book," "the reading process," elements of the "literary and linguistic," and "awareness about cultures other than their own" (p. 1).

The Librarian of Basra

Many Indonesian preservice teachers felt personally connected to the story of Alia, *The Librarian of Basra*, who orchestrated a civilian effort to rescue the vast collection of Basra library. They admired Alia's courage in risking her life to save books. One preservice teacher stated, "I love Alia. I can't believe people would be willing to save books in a library when they are in danger, but Alia is different. She is a book lover. She loved books more than she loved herself. That's amazing!"

Alia's story appeared to reflect parts of themselves and thus served as a *mirror*—a *mirror* is a term pioneered by Rudin Bishop—in which they "see something of themselves in the text" (Tschida, Ryan, & Ticknor, 2014, p. 29). Many preservice teachers used Alia as a point of reference to ponder about themselves.

Another preservice teacher admitted:

> Honestly, I don't like to read books because I think reading books is a burden. I want to read a book for pleasure, but I can't feel that way. I always carry a book with me for a course assignment, but I don't know how eager I am to read the book unless I have a deadline to finish it. But I really envy Alia. She regards books as her best friend. She carries them with her everywhere, and she tries to keep her books safe even though there is a war in her country. Books are everything to her. It changed my perspective about books. Books are important whether I like it or not. Books can be my best friend or my burden depending on my perspective about books themselves. Now I believe that loving books is the way to see the world.

Alia's story seemed to give the preservice teachers more positive attitudes toward reading.

The participants' responses also included the importance of international literature, particularly a story from a perspective that is different from the mainstream. Many preservice teachers found Alia's story refreshing because the book tells a true story from a Muslim perspective, which is usually negatively portrayed by the global mass media. One preservice teacher said:

> This story was based on a true story. I found something new. Usually, "English" is always related to "the Western culture" but in this story, the author used Muslims as the story's main character, and Basra, a city in Iraq, as the story's setting.

Being Muslims themselves, many preservice teachers felt personally connected to the positive description of a Muslim character and hoped others could take the good things from the book.

Main characters of Muslim background are hard to find in the children's literature market. The author testifies to this as she only held a children's book featuring Muslim main characters (*Does My Head Look Big in This?* a novel by Randa Abdel-Fattah) for the first time when she was an international graduate student studying children's and young adult literature in an American university. Raised as a Muslim, the author felt in that moment that her faith and tradition were validated and represented in the mainstream story.

Indonesian Muslims most often see Muslim characters in the mainstream culture from Western movies and other visual products, and the characters are usually depicted negatively and most often seen with suspicion. In Indonesia it is hard to find English books that portray Muslim main characters whose faith and appearance are relatable to Muslim readers. English children's publications that have been translated in Indonesia include popular books such as Jeff Kinney's (2007) *Diary of a Wimpy Kid*, Enid Blyton's (1997) *The Famous Five*, and J. K. Rowling's (1997) *Harry Potter* series. English books whose main characters are nonwhite, let alone Muslim, are hard to find in Indonesia.

Muslims in Indonesia follow the Sunni tradition. They practice religious rituals and traditions that resemble those being practiced in most Muslim populations in the Middle East. The Shias, another Islamic tradition that populates Iraq, make up a tiny group in Indonesia, and their existence is hardly noticeable in public.

This fact of Muslims in Iraq consisting of Sunni and Shite groups did not become a point of consideration when the Indonesian preservice teachers read *The Librarian of Basra*. Rather, the preservice teachers embraced the story and felt their Muslim identity being represented somewhat by the character of Alia. Alia represents a figure who is missing from their reading of English books. Alia is the character who drives the story, and her courage is demonstrated when she rescues books from the library in danger of destruction from war.

The Indonesian preservice teachers unanimously agreed that a love of books is good. However, many of them confessed that they were not too fond of reading. Reading *The Librarian of Basra* seemingly gave the participants a mirror into their own lives and provided them with empowered feelings. In the story, the preservice teachers saw a Muslim character whose qualities they admired. In other words, Alia's brave acts empowered them.

They also found the story special because it was based on a real story published in a newspaper. The notion that news or facts can be presented in such a compelling way, as in *The Librarian of Basra*, appeared to be a new revelation for the Indonesian preservice teachers.

Books available in Indonesian schools are predominantly textbooks and short stories published by the government. The texts are usually centered on friendship, respecting elders, and developing good traits such as perseverance and politeness. They carry normative messages, such as an obedient child will be successful in life. Picture books of high quality like those in advanced countries are not yet common in Indonesia.

The preservice teachers in this study gained new knowledge about the *literature genre*: specifically, the information/nonfiction picture book. One participant stated, "One thing that made me surprised was that news could be used by a brilliant author as story in a picture book."

The preservice teachers began to see that there was much they could do with nonfiction picture books like Alia's story. Another preservice teacher noted: "I can learn about history and art. Even if I don't travel much, through nonfiction picture books I can learn about other countries." For many preservice teachers, this picture book, more than others, seems to have inspired them to write their own stories. One of them declared, "The story's lesson inspired me to become a writer someday."

Of Thee I Sing: A Letter to My Daughters

One intriguing detail in the Indonesian preservice teachers' response to Obama's *Of Thee I Sing: A Letter to My Daughters* was how much they felt connected to the book. Unlike *The Librarian of Basra* where they felt connected to the story on a personal, possibly religious level, their connection to *Of Thee I Sing* refers to inspirational human qualities such as courage, empathy, and selflessness. The preservice teachers felt inspired by Obama's message to his daughters and were moved by the history of black Americans in the country.

The preservice teachers found the stories in Obama's book *inspiring*. They said, "The story was so interesting. Barack Obama tells his daughters that they are so special that they could be anything they want to be in this life. This book is the kind of inspirational and motivational book that I like." One figure from the book who drew the most attention was Abraham Lincoln and his dedication to abolish slavery.

They also focused on the character's intention as a way to make sense of the story. At times, they did so by extending the original text and drawing more information from other sources. Within the story of Abraham Lincoln, the participants listened to the part of the text that describes Abraham Lincoln as a man who "kept our nation one and promised freedom to enslaved sisters and brothers" (p. 28).

After discussing the book, one preservice teacher named Yanto wrote in his journal:

> Obama's message resonated with me because I'm also very impressed with what Lincoln did for Black American citizens. He fought for Black Americans' rights to live as free human beings. He stated that Black Americans had the same right to live as other citizens. Lincoln fought tirelessly, until he finally got assassinated. Fortunately, he finally succeeded to set Black Americans free. As a result, now Obama has become the president of the USA. (Obama 2010, p. 28)

Yanto's comment suggests his connection to the story about Abraham Lincoln. He admired Lincoln's crusade against slavery, which seems to have sparked his sense of humanity and justice. Yanto's responses obviously extended the original text. He talked about black Americans and the Civil Rights Movement, topics that were not explicitly mentioned in the original text. His comment was perhaps in part a result of our discussions about Obama during the read-aloud session. The class indeed had a discussion about the history of slavery and black Americans, and that discussion seemed to have contributed to Yanto's response to the book.

(MIS)INTERPRETATION OF THE STORIES FROM OTHER CULTURES

The previous sections described the Indonesian preservice teachers' responses to the stories from foreign cultures. To a great extent, the information provides insight into some shared student responses when reading stories from cultures different from their own. Continuing an effort to further our understanding about their responses to the international stories that are unfamiliar to them, this section will provide findings that appear to be their misreadings of the stories from China, Iraq, and the United States.

Gender. In reading *Yeh-Sen: A Cinderella Story from China*, the Indonesian preservice teachers seemed to compare the book to Disney's film version. They were bewildered by the story contents that departed from the Disney version they had already known. In particular, they were perplexed with the story's illustrations because some did not match their expectations. Some muttered that the illustrations looked different, and this meant to me that they were different from the more familiar Disney version.

A scene in which the prince peeks at Yeh-Shen is one example. The prince wears a turban and a pair of earrings. It took some time for the preservice teachers to realize that the image belonged to a man, and in particular, the prince. They needed to read the text twice to match the text and the story line with the image before they finally agreed that it was the illustration of the prince. The preservice teachers seemed to have previously formed an idea of how a prince should look. In Disney's *Cinderella*, the prince neither wears a turban nor earrings, and most participants said that they were familiar with Disney's *Cinderella*.

During the classroom discussion, the preservice teachers mentioned that earrings, in their view, are not commonly worn among men. This suggests a certain expectation of a male and a female fashion norm in Indonesia. Ed Young's authentic illustration of the prince invokes the ancient tradition of China. However, the Indonesian preservice teachers who were unfamiliar with ancient Chinese culture and perhaps influenced by Disney's version had certain expectations of fashion and gender and could not easily recognize the representation of a Chinese man.

This type of misreading with regard to the expectations of fashion and gender appears again when reading *The Librarian of Basra*. The preservice teachers debated at length an image of a person riding on a boat near the story's end. They wondered whether the figure belonged to a man or a woman and were puzzled by the figure's turban and long dress, an outfit that is similar to the clothes that Alia, the story's female main character, wears.

The Indonesian preservice teachers' misreadings concerning the illustrations of the two stories above seemed to be influenced partly by one, an expectation related to gender, and two, a familiarity to a particular depiction of the *Cinderella* story.

Their expectation about a clear gender distinction is evidenced in their long debate over *The Librarian of Basra*'s wordless page featuring a figure wearing a long garment. Moreover, their familiarity with Disney's *Cinderella* story seemed to be having an effect on their expectation about images typically depicted in an illustration, as in the case with the prince in *Yeh-Shen: A Cinderella Story from China*. Disney's *Cinderella* seemed to serve as a point of reference to what was considered typical in terms of the narrative details—in this case, how a prince ought to be depicted in an illustration.

For the Indonesian preservice teachers, the prince's appearance in *Yeh-Shen* differed from Disney's standard. Additionally, to some extent, their comments about the prince's earrings revealed that the depiction in *Yeh-Shen* was confusingly feminine.

Religion. In *The Librarian of Basra*, Alia's challenge when rescuing the library books mainly came from the indifferent responses from both Iraq and Western soldiers—both camps were unresponsive when Alia expressed her concern and sought help. The participants' misreading from *The Librarian of Basra* occurred when they assumed that the threats against the library came only from the Western soldiers. One preservice teacher explicitly said that the United States caused the war.

At that time, I asked the participant to provide evidence for such a claim, and he responded that he had heard this statement from the news. I observed that this prejudicial attitude originated from mixed feelings toward the West, especially to the United States as the superpower. On one hand, most participants regard the United States highly in terms of quality of life and good education. Many aspire to get scholarships to US graduate schools. On the other hand, they tend to blame the United States for tragedies in Muslim-populated countries such as Iraq.

Following the invasion of Iraq in 2003, many Indonesians critically viewed the United States regarding a unilateral decision made without approval from the United Nations. Like many Muslims in other countries (e.g., Turkey), Indonesians had a strong opinion that the American invasion of Iraq was motivated more by its interests in Middle East oil resources rather than by its official intention to seize weapons of mass destruction and to combat terrorism (Holsti, 2008).

The Librarian of Basra scarcely discusses the context of the Iraq War (the fact that the American-led army invaded Iraq and toppled Sadam Hussein's regime); the illustrations are the only indication of the two groups, the Iraq and Western armies.

The preservice teachers' reading, however, seemed to overlook the Iraqi army (who in the story is portrayed as unhelpful and equally terrifying to Alia). Instead, they seemed to fixate on the Western soldiers. To some extent, their reading was partially driven by prejudice; that is, they had an assumption before evidence in reading. In fairness, though, their prejudice came from their understanding that it was indeed the Western soldiers who invaded Iraq.

Representation. In reading *Of Thee I Sing: A Letter to My Daughters*, the Indonesian preservice teachers were faced with some challenges regarding how to access a story that is arguably unique to American culture and history.

For sure, they were quite familiar with the name *Obama*, particularly because Obama spent some childhood years in Indonesia. Albeit lacking specific details, they had some awareness about Obama's two daughters and the context of his open letter to them. In other words, the lack of background knowledge the preservice teachers had about American history and the important characters of the book contributed to their lack of understanding about the stories told in *Of Thee I Sing*.

For instance, the preservice teachers had a difficult time figuring out a poetic meaning behind each prominent character (e.g., Sitting Bull, the healer "man who healed broken hearts and broken promises" [p. 12]). The preservice teachers commented on an unusual illustration of Sitting Bull (a configuration of nature). It is important to recognize that a widely held perception among the Indonesian preservice teachers is that most known American figures are predominantly white, with the exception of an internationally known figure, such as Martin Luther King.

This is evident, for instance, when they read about other American historical figures like Jackie Robinson. The text describes, "Have I told you that you are brave?" (p. 10). The illustration of Jackie Robinson shows the baseball legend in uniform as he swings a baseball bat. The preservice teachers identified the figure plainly as a baseball player, not a legend. They seemed perplexed with the text that asks, "Have I told you that you are brave?"

When the word *brave* is narrated alongside Jackie Robinson's image, the association between the word and the legend appeared to be finally clear. The preservice teachers associated the word *brave* with Jackie Robinson's decision to become a professional baseball player in the all-white baseball arena of his time.

This is perhaps due to the Indonesian preservice teachers' lack of prior knowledge about Jackie Robinson's prominence in postslavery American history.

This particular reality increasingly became evident when they considered the word *brave* versus the word *strong*, which was used to describe Helen Keller, a deaf-blind activist who appeared to be familiar among the Indonesian preservice teachers. When they discussed "strongness" in Helen Keller, they were rather at ease discussing the meaning of "strongness" in Keller's case. One preservice teacher said, "The word 'strong' in Keller refers to being strong when facing life challenges," which illustrates that the preservice teachers understood that the word meant beyond physical strength.

It seemed that the preservice teachers associated Jackie Robinson's bravery with physical ability only, whereas "strong" in Keller was associated with mental strength. Their take on the meaning of the same words confirms the earlier suggestion about the insufficient knowledge on the part of the Indonesian preservice teachers about the history of slavery in the United States, particularly events associated with postslavery struggles.

EMPOWERMENT AND LACK OF REPRESENTATION

Responding to the stories from foreign cultures (China, Iraq, and the United States), the Indonesian preservice teachers showed their personal connections to the stories. They felt deeply connected to Alia, a Muslim female librarian in *The Librarian of Basra*, who performed the heroic act of saving books from the Iraq War when she ignored threats against her life made by combat soldiers from both Iraq and Western countries.

They also felt connected to the story from the United States (*Of Thee I Sing*). Unlike Alia, whose connection indicated their having a connection (mirrors) with a character whose religious identity they shared, their connection to Obama's story was a feeling that was inspired from the message. They were inspired by the story; thus, the story served as *windows*—another term coined by Rudin Bishop (Tschida, Ryan, & Ticknor, 2014)—that offered the participants a chance to view the worlds and experiences of others from others' perspectives.

Reading the foreign stories also ignited their curiosity, particularly their keen attention to the illustrations and the significance of symbols in *Yeh-Shen: A Cinderella Story from China*. The symbols especially reminded the preservice teachers of other customs such as feet binding to create small female feet practiced in China up until the middle of the twentieth century.

The preservice teachers' responses to these foreign stories, however, also showed some misreadings.

Gender was one of them. They were confused about the illustration of figures who wear certain cultural outfits. In *Yeh-Shen*, for instance, the preservice teachers wondered about the gender identity of a figure who wears earrings. A similar reading attitude also occurred in *The Librarian of Basra* in which the preservice teachers wondered about the gender of a figure in a boat who wears a long garment. In the case of *Yeh-Shen*, their confusion seems to have been influenced by their familiarity with *Cinderella* story characters depicted in Disney films.

It seems their gender bias and Disney's influence combined to trigger their confusion.

The Indonesian preservice teachers appeared to differentiate male and female figures by looking at the clothes they wear—looking for what was considered standard and acceptable to wear in public in Indonesia. This perhaps was a reflection of what the larger Indonesian society expects to see, a topic that perhaps rarely becomes an issue in the United States.

Take, for example, the dress code at the university where this study took place. The university expects its students to conform to an Islamic dress code while on campus and reinforces this code for appropriate fashion by displaying a large picture of a male figure who wears pants and a buttoned-up, long-sleeved shirt and a female figure who wears a long blouse with a headscarf.

To some extent, this dress code reflects the society that influences the Indonesian preservice teachers' perceptions about gender and fashion. Therefore, they could have been unconsciously influenced by what was visible and deemed acceptable Islamic dress for females and males and by the fashion seen in Disney films as well.

The preservice teachers' misreading was also found in *The Librarian of Basra* when they were unanimous in pointing to the Western soldiers as the (only) bad people in the story—despite the author's effort to suggest that looming threats to the librarian, Alia, came from both from the Iraqi and the Western soldiers. The prior information about the US-led invasion into Iraq appears to have contributed to their quick judgment.

However, it is also possible that being Muslims themselves, the Indonesian preservice teachers showed more favorable attitudes toward the Iraqi soldiers who are also Muslims. Their favorable bias toward Muslims in general seems to be a reasonable result in the absence of stories that depict Muslims favorably.

Overall, when the Indonesian preservice teachers can have a personal connection to a story, their comprehension increases because they feel sympathetic and empathetic toward the characters.

The Librarian of Basra showed a positive representation of a Muslim character usually missing from their reading. Being Muslim, the Indonesian preservice teachers might have felt empowered by the heroic depiction of the main character in the story. The preservice teachers' Muslim identity could have been positively impacted when they encountered the story of Alia, a strong (albeit rare) Muslim role model.

Thus, the depiction encouraged hope of Muslim characters being positively portrayed in an English book. This was evident from their comments that they found a genuine love of books. In other words, the scarcity of Muslim children's books caused their favorable reading.

In reading *Of Thee I Sing*, the preservice teachers showed a stance that is connected to a humanistic and universal message about courage and selflessness. They were inspired by the stories in the book. However, there was a limit to such connection, especially to the stories rarely told to readers outside the United States, as in the case of Jackie Robinson and Sitting Bull. With a lack of background knowledge about American history regarding Native Americans, slavery, and the Civil Rights Movement, their comprehension of foreign stories such as *Of Thee I Sing* was visibly inadequate.

The preservice teachers' misreadings indicated that the dominance of white characters and a lack of minority characters in the books available in English significantly affected how they interpreted the stories. A lack of diverse characters in English books could invite misreadings of stories of minority figures.

The Indonesian preservice teachers rarely see and read about people other than whites in the United States. For instance, their response to Jackie Robinson's story in *Of Thee I Sing* was merely literal (presumably due to their lack of prior knowledge) compared to a thoughtful response for the more familiar Helen Keller. It seems that this lack of diverse characters in the children's books, as a consequence, affected the degree in which the preservice teachers were empathetic toward figures in the United States whose stories were rarely told in Indonesia.

CONCLUSION

The Indonesian preservice teachers' responses to the international stories described in this chapter present three important implications. First, to those whose race/ethnicity, culture, religion, and more are rarely represented in children's stories, reading stories that represent them also empowers them. We see how a Muslim character named Alia in *The Librarian of Basra: A True Story from Iraq* greatly affected the Indonesian preservice teachers who were also Muslim; the story provided them a more positive reading attitude and allowed them to envision their future selves, such as becoming a writer.

Second, a lack of minority representations in global and international children's literature may negatively affect the level of understanding of stories. We see the Indonesian preservice teachers' struggles to connect with the minority figures Sitting Bull (a Native American leader) and Jackie Robinson (the first African American professional baseball player) described in *Of Thee I Sing: A Letter to My Daughters*. For readers in Indonesia, stories about minority figures are harder to find than books that are centered on white figures (e.g., Helen Keller).

Finally, the dominance of the Western cultural framework throughout the world may skew readers' interpretations. We see that the Indonesian preservice teachers' biased reading of *Yeh-Shen: A Cinderella Story from China* indicates that their reading remains within the confines of the Western standpoint, in this case the Disney industry.

REFERENCES

Asselin, M. (2000). Confronting assumptions: Preservice teachers' beliefs about reading and literature. *Reading Psychology, 21*(1), 31–55.

Brenner, D. (2003). Bridges to understanding: Reading and talking about children's literature in teacher education. *Action in Teacher Education, 24*(4), 79–86.

Cotton, P. (2000). *Picture books sans frontiers*. England: Trentham Books.

Draper, M. C., Barksdale-Ladd, M. A., & Radencich, M. C. (2000). Reading and writing habits of preservice teachers. *Reading Horizons, 40*(3), 185–203.

Floden, R. E., & Meniketti, M. (2005). Research on the effects of coursework in the arts and sciences and in the foundations of education. In M. Cochran-Smith & K. M. Zeichner (Eds.), *Studying teacher education: The report of the AERA panel on research and teacher education* (pp. 261–308). Washington, DC: American Educational Research Association.

Holsti, O. R. (2008). *To see ourselves as others see us: How public abroad view the United States after 9/11*. Ann Arbor: The University of Michigan Press.

Kiefer, B. (2008). What is a picturebook, anyway? The evolution of form and substance through the postmodern era and beyond. In S. J. Pantaleo & L. Sipe (Eds.), *Postmodern picturebooks: Play, parody, and self-referentiality* (pp. 9–20). New York: Routledge.

Marshall, J. D. (2000). Research on response to literature. In M. Kamil, P. Mosenthal, P. D. Pearson, & R. Barr (Eds.), *Handbook of reading research* (Vol. III) (pp. 381–402). Mahwah, NJ: Erlbaum.

Mills, G. E. (2007). *Action research: A guide for the teacher researcher* (3rd ed.). Upper Saddle River, NJ: Pearson.

Rosenblatt, L. (2005). Viewpoints: Transaction versus interaction—A terminological rescue operation. In L. Rosenblatt (Ed.), *Making meaning with texts: Selected essays* (pp. 38–49). Portsmouth, NH: Heinemann.

Roser, N., Martinez, M., & Wood, K. (2011). Students' literary responses. In D. Lapp & D. Fisher (Eds.), *Handbooks of research on teaching the English language arts* (3rd ed.) (pp. 264–70). New York: Routledge.

Sipe, L. R. (2000). The construction of literary understanding by first and second graders in oral response to picture storybook read-alouds. *Reading Research Quarterly, 35*(2), 252–75.

Sipe, L. (2008). *Storytime: Young children's literary understanding in the classroom.* New York: Teachers College Press.

Tschida, C. M., Ryan, C. L., & Ticknor, A. S. (2014). Building on windows and mirrors: Encouraging the disruption of "single stories" through children's literature. *Journal of Children's Literature, 40*(1), 28–39.

Wolf, S. A. (2001). "Wax on/wax off": Helping preservice teachers "read" themselves, children, and literature. *Theory into Practice, 40*(3), 205–11.

Wolf, S. A., Ballertine, D., & Hill, L. (2000). Only connect!: Cross cultural connections in the reading lives of preservice teachers and children. *Journal of Literacy Research, 32*(4), 533–69.

CHILDREN'S BOOKS CITED

Abdel-Fattah, R. (2008). *Does my head look big on this?* New York: Scholastic.

A-Ling, L (1982). *Yeh-Shen: A Cinderella story from China.* Illustrated by E. Young. New York: Philomel Books.

Blyton, E. (1997) *The famous five.* London: Hodder Children's Books.

Kinney, J. (2007*). Diary of a wimpy kid.* New York: Amulet Books.

Obama, B. (2010). *Of thee I sing: A letter to my daughters.* Illustrated by L. Long. New York: Alfred. A. Knopf.

Rowling, J. K. (1998*). Harry Potter and the sorcerer's stone.* New York: Scholastic.

Winter, J. (2005). *The librarian of Basra: A true story from Iraq.* Orlando, FL: Harcourt.

About the Editors

Daniel Miles Amos was the first US graduate student to successfully complete ethnographic research in the People's Republic of China. He has been professionally affiliated with several universities in Asia and the United States, including the Chinese University of Hong Kong, Beijing Normal University, Wuhan University, Clark Atlanta University, and the University of Washington. Currently, he is a Fulbright Scholar completing research in Hong Kong.

Yukari Takimoto Amos, a native of Japan, is a professor of multicultural education and TESL at Central Washington University. She has published journal articles, book chapters, and books on a wide range of subjects. Her research has included studies of Asian international students, teacher candidates of color, critical race theory, and ESL/JSL (Japanese as a Second Language) pedagogy.

About the Contributors

Chong Eun Ahn is an assistant professor in the Department of History at Central Washington University. Her doctoral dissertation, "From Chaoxian ren to Chaoxian zu: Korean Identity under Japanese Empire and Chinese Nation-State," examines identity formation of ethnic Koreans, who were treated as colonial subjects in the Japanese Empire and then categorized as ethnic minorities in the People's Republic of China. Her academic interests include East Asian history and culture and issues of colonialism, modernity, ethnicity, labor migration, and empires.

Kathy Brashears, a former elementary teacher and principal, currently serves as a professor at Tennessee Tech University. Her research interests include cultural awareness, the Appalachian region, and literacy practices.

Tati Lathipatud Durriyah (Tati D. Wardi) is a lecturer at the Universitas Islam Negeri (UIN) in Jakarta, Indonesia. Among many courses she teaches, her favorite one is an introduction to children's literature. Her classroom-based research focuses on reader response, picture books, and digital literacy. She loves talking about books and making a deliberate effort to develop a culture of reading with her student teachers.

Sharryn Larsen Walker is a professor of literacy education at Central Washington University. Her areas of research include preservice teaching methods, children's literature, and early literacy. Currently, she is a member of the board of directors for children's literature in reading special interest group of the International Literacy Association (ILA).

Annie Yen Ning Yang received her PhD in interpersonal and intercultural communication from the University of Missouri-Columbia in 2010. As a globetrotter, she has traveled and taught culture and communication in numerous locations across four continents.

www.ingramcontent.com/pod-product-compliance
Lightning Source LLC
Chambersburg PA
CBHW021800230426
43669CB00006B/141